99

Pornucopia

Titles by Piers Anthony
Published by Mundania Press

ChroMagic Series
Key to Havoc
Key to Chroma
Key to Destiny

Pornucopia Series
Pornucopia
The Magic Fart

Dragon's Gold Series
by Piers Anthony and Robert Margroff
Dragon's Gold
Serpent's Silver
Chimaera's Copper
Orc's Opal
Mouvar's Magic

Of Man and Manta Series
Omnivore
Orn
OX

Other Titles by Piers Anthony
Macroscope
Conversation With An Ogre

PIERS ANTHONY

Pornucopia

Mundania Press

Pornucopia

A Mundania Press Production

Mundania Press LLC
6470A Glenway Ave #109
Cincinnati, Ohio 45211

To order additional copies of this book, contact:
books@mundania.com
www.mundania.com

Cover and Interior Art by Joel Mallory
Cover Design by Stacey L. King
Book Design and Edited by Daniel J. Reitz, Sr.
Production and Promotion by Bob Sanders

Trade Paperback ISBN: 0-9723670-1-2
Hardcover ISBN: 0-9723670-0-4
eBook ISBN: 0-9723670-2-0
Limited Signed Edition ISBN: 0-9723670-3-9

First Edition—December 2002
Second Edition—June 2003
Third Edition—August 2004
Library of Congress Catalog Card Number 2002114168

Production by Mundania Press LLC
Printed in the United States of America

10   9   8   7   6   5   4   3

TABLE OF CONTENTS

TABLE OF ILLUSTRATIONS

Part 1:

Smegma

Chapter 1—Succubus

The early afternoon sun beat down, warming his bathing trunks, heating his crotch. The restless tide retreated slowly, as though the ocean water were evaporating, and the shock of the breaking waves was muted—crash, splash, like the breaking of a vigorous orgasm against a taut diaphragm. Prior Gross reclined on the burning sand, squirming until it shaped to his feet, palms and buttocks. He kept his knees elevated in an awkward effort to conceal the unprovoked erection that had been trapped at half-mast beneath the unyielding cloth.

There was really no reason for it, but the tumescence refused to subside. Girl-watching here was fair-to-poor. Prior's field of vision embraced grandmothers and children with scarce nubility between, and that critically flawed by obesity, sag and blemish. He was disappointed and bored—yet his member strained valiantly against the fabric, pushing it out throb by throb, and no matter how covertly he shifted about it only aspired higher. It felt as though the glans had been caught in the crotch-netting and was too stupid to realize that it could never clear the hurdle without first slacking down a little.

A fat-bellied sun-skinned executive type ambled by, glancing at Prior. Had the busybody seen? Prior's trunks bowed out marginally farther while he fought to keep a flush from his face. He could not stand up, of course, and the proximity of a hawkeyed matron prevented him from unhooking the obstruction by hand. He suffered a mental picture of the matron lumbering across the sand to the nearest lifeguard, screaming about the indecent act that man was performing, while a crowd gathered around to look and police sirens drew nigh. No, he couldn't lay a finger on his crotch!

His eyes wandered desperately about the beach, as though he

could prevent others from watching him by watching them first. But nobody was paying him any attention, yet. He saw two toddlers playing near the water's margin, using a toy shovel and fingers to shape a crumbly sand castle. The little boy was burying his legs at the same time, scooping gouts from the wet castle wall to his sister's frustration.

Full-blown, the solution came to Prior. He could bury his legs in sand, right up past the crotch. It might seem to be a childish game, but it was not entirely out of place for any age. That would hide the pulsing bulge until the situation abated. Maybe by then it would be late enough to find some action in town, to reduce his member to a lower level of chronic readiness and spare him further embarrassments.

Prior began sweeping sand in over his feet, piling it up under his lifted knees. The surface grains were hot, but those below were cool, and the sensation on his thighs goaded his penis to even more strenuous effort. It took a lot of sand to cover him, and he quickly encountered rougher gravel below. The job promised to be tedious, particularly since there were numerous sharp shell fragments embedded in the solidly packed understratum. This was not child's-play after all. He would have slashed fingers if he didn't watch it. He tensed his jaw muscles and kept working, using the task as a mental distraction.

A shadow crossed him with a sudden soft coolness. Prior looked up to spy a phenomenal pair of legs slanting into an opaque knee-length skirt. Above that the blazing sun made vision difficult, but the silhouette was strikingly feminine. Prior's member had been showing signs of retirement, but now it tugged frantically at its anchor. There was hardly any chance the woman could overlook it.

"Building a castle?" she inquired, her voice low and sultry.

"Um," he agreed, edging his knees together. The laboriously mounded sand collapsed defiantly, uncovering the castle's main tower further.

"Let me see," she said, squatting before him and prying his knees gently apart with her cool hands.

The cloth covering his crotch rose up eagerly to stand inspection. Prior could see between her handsome, well-fleshed thighs now, inside the skirt that had slid over her knees. That firm and rounded vista was obscured only at the deepest cleft by an annoying wash of shadow.

"You don't have enough sand," she pointed out. He still couldn't make out her face because of the sun, but his eyes had adjusted enough to penetrate the shadow beneath her skirt. He saw now that her posterior was innocent of panties or other defense. Open to the breeze.

"Give me time," he said, scratching feebly for more sand. Time? Sand? He could see something else he wanted! If only this weren't happening in mid-afternoon on a public beach.

"I'll bury you," she said suggestively, and a muscle rippled inside one thigh. What legs she had! She began hauling in sand from a wider semicircle, those thighs flexing as her balance shifted, and piling the sand about his trunks. "Lie down." She patted sand about his crotch.

Lie down? It was about to launch toward the moon!

Oh—she meant *him*. Prior lay back, feeling the tension between his legs increase to the point of pain. She spilled cool sand entirely over him, patting it solicitously in key places. "You don't lie very well," she murmured. 'What's your name?"

On that score he could accommodate her. "Prior Gross."

She laughed, her bosom bouncing. She had an excellent upper torso; the lower distraction had prevented him from noticing it before. "For Priapus, god of sex! You *are* a find! No wonder I was drawn to you. I thought it was only your condition."

What did she mean by that? That she sniffed out men with erections? "How did you know? Uh, about my name." He tried to make it sound bantering, but he was curious too. She had traced his name correctly. Most people knew almost nothing of mythology, and she hardly seemed the scholarly type.

"I'm a succubus," she said matter-of-factly. "We all worship Priapus."

Prior forced a laugh of his own, though it jogged the knot in his trunks and caused the packed sand there to crack as though a miniature earthquake had passed. "A succubus! A female demon?"

"Who visits sleeping men and harvests their seed," she said. "It's all quite straightforward. When I have a good load, I transform into an incubus and go in search of female companionship. If I find a sleeping girl soon enough, I can even get her pregnant—and the man I had first is the biological father. That can lead to some interesting situations, in this age of blood typing and semen analysis."

"Artificial insemination with a vengeance." Prior said, not believing any of it but intrigued by her pose. She was obviously on the make, and he would be well satisfied to get made. "So that's why some men claimed they've been framed even when blood tests and such give them the lie. They've fornicated by proxy."

She had a fair mound of sand around him now. "I can see you don't really believe me, so I'll demonstrate. I'll knock up a girl by you, right here on the beach, right now." She moved forward to sit on his crotch, spreading her dark skirt out over the mound. Prior's member, stimulated by this suggestive pressure, was almost ready to spurt spontaneously.

"You do that," he said. What a line, and by a woman, yet. And she was structured like a centerfold. She could have her will of any man she wanted, just by showing him what she had shown Prior.

Which was suspicious. Prior was no bronzed beach bum. He generally had to pay for what he wanted—and a dish like this was way out of his price range.

"You have to be asleep," she said, touching his eyelids. "That's the law."

"What law?" He had half-expected her to demand a hundred and fifty dollars in advance.

"The demonic law. Succubi only visit sleeping men. That's our nature."

"Why are you here, then?" he demanded. Her fidgeting was really working him up. She certainly knew that part of her trade! Did she want his eyes closed so he couldn't see her take his wallet? No chance; his wallet was locked safely in his car.

She didn't answer right away. She put a hand inside her own waistband and worked it down under her skirt until her fingers touched him. She began to scrape the sand from between her legs. A neat maneuver, and somehow everything looked ordinary from outside. No one could see what her hidden hand was doing. "Things get dull in daylight."

Now her hand was finished, and he felt her touch on his tight trunks, stroking the zipper fly. He had thought he was at the peak of excitation, but this elevated it another level.

"So you thought you'd drum up a little after-hours business," he said. "But I'm not asleep." Why was he arguing? If she deserted him now, he might never abate his erection. Priapism, it was called: the perpetual rigidity. He understood that could get very uncomfortable.

"That's what I said. But if you'll just close your eyes and breathe evenly, it'll be the same. No one will know."

What the hell, he thought. They had made no agreement. She would have tough luck collecting her money *after* the performance. He closed his eyes.

"That's good." Her hidden hand worked down the zipper, opening his fly with expertise, sliding the webbing across. His penis sprang out, hurting again as the kink was finally released, but wasting no time about swelling to its full proportion.

Prior cracked open an eye apprehensively, but all was concealed beneath her skirt, which now seemed voluminous. Quite a piece of apparel that could not stretch past her knees at one time, and covered everything at another time. But of course a succubus was magic, and her skirt would be magic too. It looked as though he remained buried in sand, with the girl innocently straddling the ridge: a game people played. Some game!

"Closed," she reminded him gently, her fingers massaging his member, squeezing it for the final bit of growth. "Never can tell when the supervisor's watching."

Some supervisor! Was it an invisible satyr, calibrating indexes of performance on an abacus? But Prior obliged. Actually, there was nothing to see; even her full breasts were chaste from this angle.

There was something to *feel*, though. Deprived of sight, his aware-ness magnified the inputs of touch. Her muscular thighs shifted, her cushiony buttocks adjusted—and warm damp flesh contacted his angled shaft. That living cleft he had glimpsed as she squatted was coming to embrace his own flesh.

But the angle was wrong. Those slick vagina lips were squeezing the sidewise length rather than absorbing the business end. He was on the verge of squirting into space—or at least into her skirt—and he couldn't use his hand to correct the contact.

But her fingers were there, lifting his pulsing rod, cupping the glans. The angle changed, the head brushed up against the lubricated channel and nudged delightedly into the hot cavity.

"When are you going to have your erection?" she inquired, piqued. "Don't you like women?"

The organ sank into the hole, or more correctly rose into it. Prior felt the lubricated closure pass the knob and encompass the shaft. Her flesh tightened about his own, rhythmically. "That's it!" he gasped.

"But that's hardly four inches! I like at least six, and can take eight. Nine in an emergency."

"Three point nine seven inches!" he whispered. "Erect."

"You mean all those emanations I picked up, all that worry about your hard-on showing, like a tower standing out for miles around ... *four inches?*"

"I have an ambitious imagination," he admitted.

"Ambitious! That's fraud!" she said crossly. "Here I thought I'd get my bore properly reamed..." She manipulated her buttocks to bring him in further. "I assumed that anyone named after Priapus—"

"That was my old man's wishful thinking." He had been through this before. "But my dong ended up just like his. Potent, but small."

She sighed, clenching him internally. "Well, too late to cry over spilt milk—not that I ever do spill any. Let's have it."

As she spoke, the muscles of her vulva contracted with singular authority, milking him compellingly. His orgasm ripped through his body like a fire through dry timbers. He climaxed at once, his hips thrusting up convulsively as his juice let fly. If he had done that in air, he could have knocked a seagull out of the sky!

The fire burned out as quickly as it had spread, leaving him breathlessly limp and warm. "Well, at least you had a fair quantity," she observed as he shuddered to a halt. "Good things sometimes do come in small packages." Her vagina still clasped him tightly, squeez-ing out the dregs and holding them as his spent penis slowly shrank. "Good to the last drop. But you really should wash your miniature more often."

"It itches when I wash it," he protested, embarrassed. Then: "How can you tell?"

"Sex is my business, you know. I can taste and measure everything that enters that vestibule. Your seed is potent enough, but your tool is small and uncircumcised, and frankly it's pretty cheesy too."

"Smegma is a natural secretion," he said. But he was chagrined. It did collect when he wasn't careful, and he hadn't been careful the past few days. Maybe that was the cause of his erection. Had he known what would happen on the beach...

His diminished penis finally slurped out of her vagina, which sealed up after the exodus as tightly as any anus after evacuation. She had not been fooling about salvaging the seed.

Chapter 2—Demonstration

"Which girl do you want to have it?" she asked seriously as she lifted off him.

For a moment his organ was open to the sky. Prior sat up hurriedly, packed in his apparatus together with an inadvertent handful of sand, and zipped up his fly. "Have what?"

"Your donation. I have to do it within half an hour, usually, or too many sperm cells die and it can't take. I don't have refrigeration capacity the way my northern cousins do. Of course their whole bodies are icy cold, which makes collection difficult except in the case of the most determined dreaming sinners, the kind who would shoot off into icebergs if they had the right sized holes in them. And her period has to be right, too. The supervisor's very finicky about such details."

"You mean you're serious about this succubus-incubus bit? It's not just a come-on?"

"Of course it's a come-on. You came; I got on," she said, making a moue. Her lips were very expressive; she probably knew how to use them in her profession, too. "Hurry up. Make a choice. Someone sleeping, of course."

He tried to call her bluff. "Don't you have to—to convert? To incubus?"

"Just watch me carefully. I can't be too obvious, obviously. People would stare, and we aren't supposed to attract attention to ourselves. Not in a business connection, anyway. A demon can get herself burned, that way. Are you going to choose?"

Prior looked about. Time had passed, and either some of the girl children had blossomed into nubility or the beach fauna had benefited from some turnover. But in his present sated state he found this interesting primarily in an intellectual way. He had no particular urge to impregnate any of the pregnable. In fact, the notion was a trifle disgusting.

Not that it would come to that. Succubi were creatures of folklore. This doll had had her fun and spun him a fairy tale while he, no fairy, had spun into *her* tail, and now he would play the game out until she broke, and maybe she never would remember what she had intended to charge him for the occasion.

"Her," he said, gesturing to the adjacent matron, now blissfully snoring as the sun cooked her flesh.

"She's too old. And ineligible. Hysterectomy. I can tell from here."

"She should be eager for it, then. And I want to see how you do it." And see *what* she did, and *if* she did, too.

"But the supervisor—"

"Your, ah, load isn't legitimate anyway, because I wasn't really asleep. So you might as well ditch it before you get in trouble for carrying contraband."

She looked angry, then shrugged. "All right, skeptic. You lie down on your side facing her and pretend to close your eyes, so no one knows you're watching. I'll set it up so you can see, but no one else can."

Prior nodded. Despite his cynicism, life stirred slightly in his loin again. He had called her bluff and she wasn't backing down; what sort of show would she put on now?

She walked away as he lay down. With each step she took she seemed to change. Her lovely broad hips became narrow, her hair shorter, her chest flatter. She paused to adjust her dress—and it was a pair of culottes or even Bermuda shorts, as much out of place on this beach as her skirt had been, but still unremarkable. Lots of people wore inappropriate clothing at the beach, and some walked the shoreline in full dress clothing.

Were there incubi among them, unsuspected? By the time she reached the supine matron, she was male. Prior had trouble believing this, but his eyes were quite positive about it.

The incubus knelt beside the woman as though asking her a question. No one on the beach paid attention except Prior. The incubus then moved over casually until he was astride the woman, and still no one noticed and she did not wake. He must have put a small sleep-spell on her; no doubt incubi (and succubi, of course) had dependable ways to keep their subjects passive (except sexually) for the operation. Assuming such magical creatures really existed. Assuming that this was one such. Prior was still alert for some deception, though his disbelief was somewhat shaken. If what he had seen was a trick, it was one hell of an illusion.

Then the incubus brought out a tiny knife—or maybe it was merely a sharp fingernail—and sliced away a portion of her bathing suit, exposing the pudendum. He placed his body so that only Prior could see what was happening. Still, it could be an act, a farce, and the sleight-of-hand could not proceed much farther.

In due course the incubus opened his own apparel and brought out a massive phallic instrument. This was no trick; Prior saw it come erect while the incubus kept hands off. Had he not watched the creature every moment and been certain that no substitution had been made, Prior would not have believed this. Now he was convinced: the hungry female genitals that had sucked in his protoplasm were now aggressive male genitals eager to spew it forth again.

The incubus lowered this boom and brought it to bear on the fatty crevice between the matron's legs. It looked far too big to fit, but slowly he eased it in, pushing, stroking, sliding, jogging. The woman moaned, stirred—but the incubus touched her eyelids with one hand and she did not awaken. In fact, she was smiling. Prior wondered what dreams she might be having, half as phenomenal as the reality.

The tremendous penis hove to like a slow diesel into a tunnel, burying half its column in the tight aperture, then three quarters. Hoo!, Prior thought— that female would be sore tomorrow!

After that he couldn't see the detail because the incubus's thing blocked the view. But the motions of the merging bodies suggested that the rest of the shaft was finding or making its lodging. The woman's heavy torso shook with the impact of full penetration, and she writhed with something resembling ecstasy. Her knees came up and spread farther apart; her hands groped for the point of contact. She had probably never had so much meat inside her at one time before.

Ejaculation! The incubus plunged, withdrew, plunged again. The woman groaned aloud as the piston retreated, then she made a muffled scream as the spasm distended her. Prior was sure this orgasm dwarfed her previous experience—if, indeed, she had experienced orgasm before. That kind usually thought pleasure in sex was unpatriotic.

Meanwhile, beach activity continued. No one wondered what the strange man was doing to the sleeping woman; or maybe they just didn't care. Two girls walked by, glanced across, saw, and went on; it was none of their business. Prior realized that almost anything could happen on a public beach, including screaming rape, and nobody would react.

He glanced down at his own trunks, wherein his scant four inches throbbed with second wind. Certainly *he* was not one to bring a woman to life like that. There was no way four inches could match eight, except perhaps in endurance.

The incubus let it soak for a moment while an elderly couple walked by, then drew out the gross member. The fit was still so tight that Prior could see flesh stretching. Then the organ snapped out with a pop! that caused a passing child to glance curiously, hoping for bubble-gum. No such luck. The incubus stood up, shook off his flaccid extremity, fed it back into the shorts, and ambled away.

The matron remained as she was—legs spread wide, suit slit open at the crack, hands touching the greased labia. No one noticed except the child, who didn't care. And Prior, who had mixed emotions.

By the time the incubus reached Prior, he was female again. "The bitch had gonorrhea!" the succubus exclaimed, outraged. "Do you want to do it again?"

Prior's renovated erection abruptly died. This creature, by her own admission, was now teeming with activated venereal disease.

"I need another load, since that one was wasted on an ineligible receiver," she said. "You're handiest, since you put me up to it, though it's bound to be anemic so soon after my last collection. Now I don't mind how I get it—cunt, mouth, hand or whatever—or which form I take it in—male, female, neuter—"

"You mean you can get it as an incubus, too?" Prior was repelled and fascinated, the one feeding the force of the other. "And you have a neuter state?"

"Oh yes. Oral collection is invariably effective, and of course there's anal. Some men prefer neuters—they're like undeveloped young girls or castrates. Tastes vary. Sometimes we have to bugger the donor to get him to put out. I can show you—"

"I guess I'll donate in the normal fashion," Prior said quickly. He wasn't anxious to have that eight-inch member stirring up his twitching colon. He was dead set against buggery, anyway.

"I could suck you off," she said helpfully. "That little marvel of yours makes it easy."

"You'll take it in the pussy or not at all!" he informed her defensively. He didn't normally use lowbrow terms like that, but her condescending attitude was getting to him. "And not here. Come to my car."

She made another moue and followed him over the sand and across the weedy fringe to the parking lot. His dime had run out and there was a ticket on his windshield. He had tarried on the beach longer than originally intended. This ticket was particularly embarrassing, because he was professionally connected to the parking industry and this would look very bad on his record. Like a dentist having a rotten tooth, or a grocery manager confusing the price of beans with that of caviar—though the latter was not hard to do these days, with the prices rising so fast that beans now went for caviar prices. "Shit!" he said, employing the basest expletive he knew, wondering if the succubus would be shocked.

"We supernaturals don't have to eat," she said equably, "so we seldom have to defecate. But if that sort of thing stimulates you—"

"I meant the meter. It stuck a ticket on my car. That's a dollar fine."

"Oh, I can fix that. We fuck up machines all the time: Let me get my ass on it, here—"

"I'll pay the fine!" he cried as she hoisted her skirt and lifted one shapely leg. There were whistles from a neighboring car. "Leave it alone!"

She shrugged. "It's your dough."

"Just get in the car, why don't you!" Prior was anxious to get away before more of a crowd collected.

He drove her to a private park, certain by this time that he didn't want her at his apartment. She climbed onto the back seat, got on hands and knees, let her breasts dangle low, bared her bottom, and he mounted her from behind and jetted somewhat feebly into her up-raised aperture. She was still a luscious hunk of distaff flesh, but he had seen what he had seen, there on the beach, and knew what he knew, and it shook him up quite apart from the VD threat.

Luscious hunk? As his shrinking penis sucked loose, he realized that she had assumed the neuter form: breastless, narrow-hipped, hairless. He felt like a pederast. He didn't like pederasty. "Now you're done; get out," he said shortly.

Chapter 3—Clap

After he was rid of her he drove home and took a long morose shower, scrubbing his limp penis thoroughly. Then he dried under the air-blast and spilled wine-scented shaving lotion on it from glans to scrotum, hoping the alcohol would burn off any remaining contamination. It stung like hell, but it didn't ease his mind much.

He dialed the number of the city VD clinic and asked for a print-out on gonorrhea. He read it completely. This didn't ease his mind, either.

He had to take three happy-pills to get to sleep. And he dreamed … not happily.

He dreamed that five days had passed and the tip of his penis became inflamed. It was red and tender, at first causing irregular erections, then actual pain. When he urinated there was such intense smarting that he could not tolerate more than a few drops at a time—but there seemed to be gallons in his bladder, and they had to pour out. Then pus choked the conduit, popping out in grisly lumps when the frothing urine finally blasted its way through. The agony was hellish. There was brown blood in it now.

The pus lasted for three months, causing him to stand at the toilet for half an hour at a time without performing, then soiling his pants when he walked away with bursting bladder. He wet his bed at night, hardly noticing because of the other agony, and his constantly soaked buttocks and scrotum began to feel raw, too. He couldn't eat, couldn't sleep, couldn't work because of the viper's nest of pain in his groin. Then the inflammation began to spread.

It covered his bladder and his kidneys and his rectum, making every facet of elimination a continual torture. It invaded his prostate, his testes, his epididymis, rendering him sterile several times over, the hard way. Then it advanced to his mouth, interfering with eating, and his bones and joints, giving him arthritis. It infiltrated the lining of his body cavity and the valves of his heart. It poisoned his blood. It infected his eyes, making him painfully blind. Finally it penetrated to the membrances lining his spinal cord and the brain itself, and he knew he felt the onset of paralysis and insanity.

About then he woke up in sweat so copious he could not be certain it wasn't urine, and remembered that gonorrhea was not the worst of the venereal diseases.

It was Monday, the beginning of his four-day working week. Prior was a parking lot surveyor—the reason he had been so put out about being ticketed himself. He used a laser theodolite to resurvey parking lots and make sure their dimensions were within tolerance. Unscrupulous operators—and that meant all of them—tried to shave the size of individual spaces and the access lanes, and could get ugly when called to account. The worse the offense, the uglier they got. Some threatened him, not realizing that one of the spare lenses he carried was in fact a laser pistol. Some offered him money, not realizing that his theodolite was irrevocably bugged; they were soon out of business, and he was permitted to keep the money as a gratuity for his cooperation. He liked getting bribed, except when they used counterfeit bills. Others sent attractive young sexy parking attendants to reason with him in some remarkably convenient bedroom-like office—not realizing that his penis was less than four inches long, erect, and he was sensitive about exposing it before strangers. As his bastard boss well knew; that was why Prior had been hired over more qualified applicants for the position. Some liabilities tended to make men honest...

All week, as he measured and noted and punched out deficiency reports and accepted bribes and fended off solicitous sexpots, his mind was on his penis. It probably required the deficiency report, and no bribe could add two inches to its length, but it was the only one he had. Every time he took a leak he watched for pus and fancied he felt the beginning irritation. And there *was* irritation—but only because he washed it six times a day now and the tissues were being bleached. In the middle of some intricate measurement the little soldier would stand up, stiff as a metal spike despite its brevity, and he would wonder whether this were the first gonorrheal priapism while he tried to conceal the bulge behind his theodolite.

But nothing happened.

Two weeks later a woman brought her car in to a reserved lot while he was surveying it. He was angry, because the peripheral emanations from the atomic motor interfered with his laser. But before he could formulate some suitably cutting remark, she stepped out. He recognized her: the matron the incubus had serviced on the beach. The gonorrhea trap.

Prior said nothing to her, and she never noticed him. Instead he noted the tag number of her car. When he got home he phoned the registry department and got her name and residence. Then he located her medical file. The information was supposedly confidential, but as a state employee he knew which computer buttons to press.

What he was after, of course, was the truth about her gonorrhea. Had the succubus been trying to scare him out of sheer perversity? She was, after all, a demon, and he had dismissed her impolitely.

DOES SUBJECT HAVE VENEREAL DISEASE? he typed into the appropriate line.

NO, the answer came immediately.

Relief and anger fought for supremacy. The succubus had been lying—if in fact she was a succubus, and not just an idle woman with some devilish tricks up her skirt— and he had fallen for it. There was his anger. But he had no risk of contracting gonorrhea. There was his relief.

But computers were demons in their own fashion, and liked to torpedo unwary querists with partial truths. The files only provided the specific information requested. It was always necessary to countercheck. HAS SUBJECT EVER HAD GONORRHEA?

YES.

Oh-oh. PROVIDE DETAIL ON CASE HISTORY, LAYMAN'S TER-MINOLOGY.

It turned out that the woman had had a trial marriage a decade ago (only a decade? She must be younger than she looked.) and had contracted the disease then. She had avoided treatment because of the stigma attached, so the illness had become entrenched. She had thought the hysterectomy would clean it up, but it hadn't, and she remained a carrier.

This was the bitch the incubus had tackled. Prior had then had a second contact with the succubus. He had been exposed, all right.

But the most recent note on the case history said simply: SPON-TANEOUS CURE, COMPLETE.

Prior read and reread that note, checking its veracity and date. She had had VD—but somehow in the last two weeks the disease of a decade had aborted without treatment. Why? And since she had still had it when he ran afoul of her, why hadn't *he* come down with it?

If he hadn't. Maybe his case was taking three weeks to develop the first overt symptom.

Suddenly he had the courage to go to the VD clinic himself for a checkup. The notion that he might not have gonorrhea seemed more compelling reason to go than the notion that he had it—because of that potential stigma. And other factors.

That got him off on a familiarly unpleasant chain of imagination. He would walk into the clinic, where a bunch of big, hairy, full-crotched men would stare at his member and banter their remarks back and forth while Prior stood in the center like the victim of a keep-away game. "Hey, Joe—get a load of this! Less'n four inches and clapped!" "That so? I thought the clap didn't touch anything under the legal limit!" "Mister, you better cut this sort of thing out—" (brandishing a scalpel dangerously near his defenseless penis) "It'll stunt your growth!" "Bring in the mouse you fucked; we'll have to cure it too!" But Prior knew he was as foolish as the matron in this respect. Clinic people didn't really make such crude remarks; they only thought them.

He nerved himself and went in. Everything was quiet and private and clean and deadly serious, to his considerable relief. The clinic tested him and cleared him promptly. The medical attendant didn't even snicker at the size of his penis. Prior was not now, nor had he ever been, a victim of gonorrhea.

So he had lucked out. Ridiculous to have thought himself infected.

But he stayed well clear of the beach.

Chapter 4—Hotbox

Though Prior Gross spent many of his days on the dull job, and his nights either dreaming of sexual exploits (his penis was always double length in dreamland) or worrying about their consequences (suppose one of those dreamland dolls had the syph?), his most persistent remaining concern was inventing. At home he had a device converted from a broken-down laser theodolite and a built-up computer-guided atomic-motor fuel-injection transformer. It was supposed to be a cigarette dispenser, one that would check the approaching mouth, analyze it for taste preference and general capacity, insert an appropriate brand, and light it. When the weed had burned out, the machine would remove the butt, rinse the orifice with a sweet jet of aseptic mouthwash, and insert a new cylinder. In such fashion a person would be able to chain-smoke around the clock without ever being aware of it.

He had been tinkering with the device in spare time for three years, and mechanically it seemed perfect. He would have had it ready in half the time, had the Cancer Clinic approved his application for a research grant. But the execs at Cancer had been very obtuse about the benefits of the invention. The Heart Clinic had been even worse. One of its execs had even had to call on the services of the Tranquilizer Clinic, before Prior completed his presentation. Strange folk, these Clinic officials. It almost seemed as though they had something against smoking.

Now his device was ready, at least in prototype. But it seemed that hardly anybody smoked anymore. They preferred to absorb their drugs in more convenient ways, such as incense spiked with nicotine, caffeine, speed and pot. Since Prior did not smoke himself—he had a domineering doctor—he had no way to test the machine in the field.

He had built the better mousetrap after the barn door had robbed Peter to—well, however it went, he was out of luck. That was the story of his life.

One night as he pored over his creation, trying to think of a use for it, the succubus came again. She was every bit as shapely as before, but this time was garbed in a slitskirt super décolletage evening special that put her charms into forceful focus. No wonder she got no arguments from the sleeping men she visited on her collection rounds! But Prior wanted no part of her—particularly not the part she offered.

"How did you find out where I live?" he demanded.

"I took down your tag number, of course. I knew your address before you ever got home that night. But this was the first open date I had. There've been a lot of horny men around here recently, and right now the demon ranks are spread pretty thin."

'Well, reopen it. I don't—"

"It's open, lover. Just waiting for your entry." She hoisted her skirt delicately to show him.

Prior gulped, strongly tempted in spite of himself. "I meant the date. I'm busy."

"You must be. You're hardly horny at all tonight. But at the moment I'm long on female clients and short on males. Just give me a quick fix for the gal in polka-dot who lives down the block, and I'll be on my way." She hauled up her skirt again and draped herself spread-legged on his bed.

"The girl in polka-dot?" he asked, recognizing the description. "*She* takes an incubus?"

"She will tonight." The succubus elevated her knees, causing her cleft to open wider.

"I haven't washed in a week. I'm cheesy and under four inches erect," he pointed out. "You like six and can take eight."

"Or even nine, in a bind," she agreed. She sighed, her breasts almost flowing out of her dress, which was fashioned for support, not enclosure. "Harvesting you is something of a handicap, but there's something about your produce. I had a load from an advanced syphilitic later that night, and the spirochetes all shriveled up and died." She shook her head, and her chin almost banged a breast. "Just like that, they expired—but the sperm cells stayed fresh. There's something unnatural about that."

A succubus talking about the unnatural? Yet despite his aversion to her, Prior found his curiosity piqued. "How did you know about them dying?"

"I tasted them, of course."

He remembered. Her remarkable demonic vagina could taste and measure. "So you're VD resistant. What's that to me?" Then: "Say! That's why I never caught the clap!"

"But I'm not resistant! I pass along whatever I receive, diseases and all. That's the beauty of it. I have no curative properties. I'm only a run-of-the-furnace sex demon, after all. So it must have been your fault. Nothing like that ever happened to me before, and not since."

"*My* fault!"

"Some residue from you must have acted on the next load, changing it. So I thought I'd try you again, after the effect wore off, and see if the same thing happened." She shrugged out of her dress with a maneuver Prior couldn't follow, and lifted her legs up toward the ceiling. She had a fine looking aperture, and Prior's penis responded manfully—until he remembered again what he had seen on the beach. She might not have VD right now, but the idea of that hole forming into a phallus caused his own phallus to shrink in dismay.

"Put it right here, lover," she invited, twitching the muscles of her buttocks so that her vulva winked at him.

Prior knew how persistent she could be. She would keep after him until she got her crevice properly stuffed. How could he get rid of her without a scene that would bring the nosey landlord galumphing down the hall?

His eye fell on the cigarette dispenser. Something clicked snidely in his mind. The succubus was lying with her head away from him, tilted so that she could not see him below the general region of his waist.

"Let's have ol Lingam right up Yoni," she murmured, doing a brisk bicycle-pedaling exercise that was something to behold from this angle.

He picked up the machine and turned it on, holding it low. "Coming, lover," he said.

He tilted the business end appropriately and set the box against her half-creased buttocks.

The sensor-filament poked out and tickled her crack. "Oooh, you've been practicing!" she whispered, wriggling with delight.

The machine hummed. Prior hummed too, to conceal the noise. "You sound happy," she said. "Glad you changed your mind. Fucking can be fun, you know."

Then a slender cigar popped out and nudged into her vulva. "You don't have a full erection, though," she complained. "That's not even a four inch penetration. Come on, get it hard!"

Obligingly, the machine poked the cigar in farther. "Now you taste like tobacco! What have you been doing to that little prick?"

The machine lit the projecting end. Smoke curled aromatically up between her legs. "You're really getting hot now," she said, smiling blissfully.

"You don't know the half of it," he told her. And waited. The cigar would ordinarily have taken much longer to burn, but its deep placement brought the lighted end much closer to the nether lips that held it.

"Aren't you going to squeeze me a little?" she asked. "Not that I care, as long as your meat is fired up like this, but it is an odd technique."

Prior mumbled something reassuring, his eye on the advancing glow. He began to experience apprehension. How did demons react to hotfoots in their cracks?

By and by she hit the ceiling, almost literally.

"Hot box," Prior remarked as she bounced down. Was that a set of footprints in the plaster up there?

The cigar shot out of her cleft and threw sparks against the rug as it bounced and rolled. The succubus took a moment to assess what had happened, rubbing her crotch vigorously. "You shithead pekkernosed pimpsucker," she said. Then she worked up to some ugly language.

By the time she got her first impressions out of her demonic spleen, she had converted to the male form. The incubus advanced on Prior, his monstrous penis projecting like a cannon. "I'm going to fuck your asshole right into your gizzard!"

"You can't," Prior said, backing away nervously. She was certainly overreacting, but the threat put an unholy fear into him. She? *He. It* was overreacting. "I'm not asleep, so your supervisor would object."

"It's supe's night off. He's fucking herself blind on sperm whale oil, so I can do what I want."

So an incubus/succubus could fuck himself! That would have been intriguing to contemplate, at another time. 'Well, you don't have a load on yet."

"There's some stale stuff left over from last night. What did you think you were doing, ramming a lighted weed up my cunt?"

Prior eyed the menacing phallus with increasing apprehension. He had hoped she would go away mad. She was mad, but not going away. He had miscalculated.

"It's an invention. A—" Here he had a flash of sheer genius. "A tampon machine!"

"You shrimpcocked idiot! I'm a demon! A supernatural creature. I don't have periods. I never have the rag on." But the incubus paused. "What was it doing with a *cigar*?"

"I ran out of tampons."

The incubus pondered. His ferocious erection drooped slightly. "Oh, all right. We'll call it a nicotine dildo with a live fuse and forget it. Just don't do it again. Now let's finish our business."

Prior watched as the massive member shrank into itself and the flat male breasts swelled. It was as though the substance was being siphoned from the lower torso to the upper. Finally the penis was a mere button, no larger than a clitoris. In fact, it *was* the clitoris. Meanwhile the scrotum sucked up and became an empty sac, a flap, a wrinkle of skin, and finally a concavity. Prior was now looking at the lips of the vagina, and knew that the deep aperture was forming between them.

How convenient. The succubus received the semen in her inverted scrotum. When she changed into the incubus, it was right there. Probably her ovaries became his testicles—if the demon had need of either.

Somehow Prior's own genital remained quiescent. He had no slightest urge to entrust his precious penis to that demonic grinder again, or to let this spook retail his ejaculate. Not even to the polka-dot girl, who was a fetching number.

"Come on, come on!" the succubus said impatiently. "And I do mean 'come.' You aren't the only cock of the morn."

"I'm rather busy with my tamponer," he said. "Research and development, you know." Would the Hygiene Clinic be interested enough to bestow a grant?

"Well, I'm busy with my researches too," she countered. "I want to know whether your jism cures VD or not." She backed against the bed and sat down.

On the now-upright machine.

Water squirted as the after-smoke rinse started. "Mouthwash!" she screamed indignantly. "It fucked me with mouthwash!"

Prior grabbed her in time to prevent her from smashing the tamponer. She immediately exerted her sex appeal on him, trying for a sneak collection, while he tried to escape.

In this moment of crisis he suffered his second consecutive flash of genius. "We can test them both out—box and juice—on the slots!"

She considered. "Very well. For now. The night is yet young."

Chapter 5—Slots

She dressed, her dress magically flowing to her and enfolding her. He changed, and they both adjourned to a drugstore for a box of tampons and thence to the corner coin bordello. Here there were half-stalls in a row, each with its fleshy display and listed price. The most elegant cost six tokens; the cheapest was one token.

Prior brought out his credit voucher and bought a dozen tokens. This set him back, at present exchange rates, about sixty dollars. Not a major expense, but not chickenfeed either, for one experimental session.

"That won't go far," the succubus remarked.

"Far enough on the one-per slots," he pointed out. "Those are the VD slurps, after all. From two-tokens up they're inspected, and the fives and sixes are guaranteed germfree."

"That so? I never patronized a coinery before. Not in my line."

"You might consider it. Those are real whores in the booths, you know, mostly. Apart from the animals and machines, I mean. Figure it out. In the first place, it's completely anonymous; nothing but the business end ever shows. In the second place, it's concentrated action. A girl can get serviced maybe ten times an hour with normal traffic, ten hours a day. Even an average three-toke ass can make three or four hundred dollars a shift. That's not bad pay at all."

"What use have I for money?" she asked disdainfully.

"But she gets a load each time; too. You could store up a week's worth, just like that."

"No go. I have to pass it along as I get it, or it loses its potency. One shot at a time."

"Maybe you could have two booths. Then when you get one load, you shift to a male-booth and dole it out at another couple tokens per squirt. You could go through your whole evening's business in less than an hour. If you don't want the money, give it to me. I'm natural, not supernatural; I have to eat to live."

"I'll think about it," she said, intrigued.

They walked by the higher-priced models of the female section. Each booth contained a pair of buttocks projecting from the wall, the distaff genitalia plainly visible. About half were occupied: men stood against them, flies open, organs pumping. The more expensive stands had armholes, so that the customer could reach through and fondle or abuse the breasts and torso while thrusting, and the six-toke booths were partially transparent when activated so that the prosperous client could even see what he was doing.

Prior stopped by the first of the cheapies. The buttocks were plump—grossly so. The cleft was hardly visible, being buried beneath overlapping avoirdupois even in this flexed position. There were pimples, and the crevice was creasy. Perhaps it was only sweat—but there was a good chance that it was the flow from venereal sores.

Prior reached out gingerly and tried to spread the fleshy masses to verify this. They resisted. They were surprisingly hard, as though glazed. A sign lit, above: ONE TOKEN.

He drew out a token and pressed it edgewise between those mounds. There was a click as it entered the slot set in the anus; the disk vanished, something gulped, and the buttocks relaxed. Another sign came on. YOU HAVE THREE MINUTES.

"Well, shove it in!" the succubus said. "A four minute fuck is too long; you see the sign."

Prior did not want to admit that he still had no erection, and was unlikely to get one at this stop. This fat ass was repulsive. "But I'm not sure it's infected! If I shoot my wad and there's no VD to begin with—"

"I'll check it for you," she said impatiently. She poked a finger into the cleavage and slid it along the blubbery labia until it entered the sunken hole.

"Don't play with it!" a muffled voice cried from behind the wall. "Fuck it! That's what it's there for!" It was the owner of the ponderous derrière.

The succubus ignored this intemperate outburst. She swished her long-nailed finger inside and brought it out dripping. She touched her tongue to it. "Neat's-foot oil," she announced.

"What?"

"Neat's-foot oil. Old standby to soften saddles and shoe leather."

"Saddle soap?" Prior gaped but saw she was serious. "It figures. A one-toke slot gets a lot of rough action. Probably has to be lathered up right or it hardens and cracks."

"Fuck it, eunuch!" the muffled voice pleaded.

"All in good time, ass," the succubus snapped, slapping a buttock.

"But does it have VD?" Prior demanded.

"No."

"Then we'd better try the tamponer," he said with relief.

"That's right! I forgot."

YOU HAVE THIRTY SECONDS TO COMPLETE YOUR BUSI-NESS, the sign warned.

"What happens if you don't finish in time?" the succubus asked, curious.

"It freezes up, and anything in there is stuck. Then you have to pay again, or have the fairy janitor pry you loose."

"Clever!" She shoved the box against the buttocks.

The filament came out and performed its exploration. "Stop that!" the muffled voice cried angrily. "Quit tickling and fuck it, you fuckin' impotent!"

A cigarette emerged and found loose lodging. "You forgot to stock it with those tampons you bought!" the succubus exclaimed, smiling. She evidently found humor in the situation, now that she was not the victim.

VIOLATION, the sign said, and a red flag popped up. The labia and buttocks closed around the cigarette and stiffened as though instant rigor mortis had set in. Any dawdling penis would have been in sorry straits.

"Serves you right, slowpoke!" the muffled voice chortled, thinking it *was* a pinioned penis.

Undismayed, the machine lit the cigarette, doused its light, and closed up shop.

"Let's get out of here," Prior said, seeing the weed glow slowly down toward the oiled flesh. "Does neat's-foot oil burn? There could be an explosion. The management might not approve."

"Serves her right," the succubus said smugly.

They moved on to the next unoccupied booth. This offering was sunny side up, the spread thighs disappearing at an angle into the wall above. Prior found the coinslot and pressed in a token.

"Doesn't it stretch those twats?" the succubus inquired.

"No more than a turd does. The tokens aren't that big, and the mechanism is self-contained and shaped to the bowel. The same unit injects the flesh-stiffener and its antidote. A very efficient setup."

"I'd still call it dirty money," she muttered. "The management must have a ball collecting and counting it."

The vagina came alive. The succubus inserted her finger again and sampled it. "Jackpot! Syphilis!"

Prior's member acted as though he were turning into a succubus himself. He didn't like the sound of this. "Are you sure my—that it works on syph, too?"

"Of course I'm not sure! That's why we're here! If you die of syphilis

I'll be generous enough to admit my theory was wrong."

Prior couldn't debate that reasoning, though somehow he was not reassured. He brought out his penis, and it tried to elude his grasp and hide. He hauled it out again, and it dangled like a decapitated snake. He massaged it, trying to work it into a suitable erection. The organ inflated only to half-mast, then began to subside.

"Hurry it up!" the succubus said. "Time is money."

"I thought you didn't care about money."

"I don't; you do. Get your midget pekker into the soup!"

But it shriveled like an embarrassed worm until it was largely absent. The VIOLATION sign came on.

"Oh for pity's sake!" she said. "Here—I'll take care of it. Come on over to the arcade section."

She led him to the sexview stalls, his fly still open and his little penis peeping out pitifully. No one noticed. The succubus seemed pretty knowledgeable for a creature who had never patronized a place like this.

Here, for a token, men and women could assimilate three-dimensional stereophonic odoriphorous semitactile eroticism.

Each item was rated on a sliding scale: guaranteed to bring a person to spontaneous climax within a specified period. If it failed to do so, his token was refunded. Of course he had to submit his genitals to a quick machine inspection to verify that his gun had not been fired within the past half hour, and the offer was void if certain suppressant drugs were employed. Men had been known to try to beat the machine by injecting Novocain into their erectile tissue to deaden all sensation. (It didn't work; the climactic stimulus acted on the brain, not the meat.)

Of course it was rumored that a sensitizing drug was injected by the arcade machine during its check for desensitizing drugs—but hardly anybody worried about that. An orgasm was an orgasm, after all, and a sexview orgasm was mighty good regardless.

Prior rammed in his token with more authority than his penis evinced, and passed inspection. He donned the helmet, settling the binoculars over his open eyes, the headphones over his ears, the nosecone over his nose, and the tactile band over his forehead and the back of his neck. The tape came on and the timer started.

The succubus watched his penis climb rapidly and achieve full turgidity. It quivered and thrust toward the collection basin, on the verge of detonation, while Prior's open mouth gasped and drooled. There was obviously quite a show going on in his head! Fifteen seconds had passed; five to go. (The price rose exponentially for emissions within twelve seconds, or for males under thirteen, or for frigid women.)

As the fit came over him, she hoisted her skirt, turned her torso about, and jammed her thirsty cavity onto the short pole, receiving the full ejaculation. It was a large one—a dozen jets—showing that he hadn't been tapped in some time. She smiled with satisfaction as she eased off the perch.

Prior removed the helmet. "Whew! That was so real it felt real!" Then he noted her position and remembered what they had come for. "You—did you—"

"Next time I incubate," she said as she straightened out, "I'm going to try one of those shows. This one sure lifted your counter-weight."

"Incubate?" He was still groggy from the sexview presentation. Whoever had authored the script for the sequence he had just experienced must have had a hot jock and a sick mind. It was potent stuff!

"I'm succubating at the moment."

"Oh." Obviously. Apparently she didn't have to change sexes the moment she got her load on; she could do it at her convenience.

She set off for the slot section, metamorphosing in full stride. Still dazed, he followed her ... him. Incubating, yes.

The incubus took a token and shoved it into the slot they had visited before. His gesture in doing so was obscene. As the buttocks loosened and the crack opened he plunged his eight-incher into the hole with a loud slurp. As he delivered Prior's load, he pinched the buttock with fingernails that resembled an old-time can-opener.

"Stop that!" screamed the owner's voice. "Go to the pervert department, you sadist!"

"I have just put my brand on this hair-pie," the incubus said matter-of-factly, withdrawing his spent tool. Even flaccid, it remained large. Prior stifled a siege of envy. "Or this harpy; maybe that version is better. So we'll know whether remission occurs."

Sure enough, a mystic symbol was now evident on the reddened skin. There would be no problem identifying this exhibit. Meanwhile, he agreed: hairpie equated nicely with harpy.

"Now I'll just go test out the sexviewer," the incubus said. "Take care of your box." He handed the tamponer back and walked away.

"You can't use it right after you've spurted—the guarantee's void!" Prior called. But the incubus was already out of hearing. Well, maybe he'd succubate, then try the show. Or maybe he had ways to fuck up this type of machine, too, just as she had been ready to do for the parking meter at the beach.

Prior's attention was attracted downward by the passing snicker of a ten-year-old girl. His spent penis was still hanging out, and the box's filament was nuzzling it.

He whipped his organ out of the way. He had no hankering to have a tampon rammed up it. Or a lighted cigarette.

Chapter 6—Party

Two weeks later the demon was back. Prior had almost succeeded in putting her/him out of his mind, and he had long since had himself checked out again at the VD clinic and pronounced clean. (He hadn't actually had contact with the infected slot, but you couldn't be too careful about a thing like that.) He had not washed his penis in five days, and was feeling much more comfortable in the mundane world. He had perfected his tamponer by eliminating the cigarette-lighting feature—tampons did not burn evenly anyway—and modifying the filament and rinse. He expected to make his fortune momentarily.

"It didn't work," the succubus said. "That slot still has the clap."

"She never had the clap," he pointed out. "That means gonorrhea, not syphilis."

"Details," she muttered. "Your jism didn't jizz, regardless. She's as VD'd as ever."

"So? You were the one who made the claim. I never thought my produce was premium grade. I'm just glad I never dunked my own tender flesh in that slot-cesspool."

"There's still *something*. Maybe you radiate curative rays or something. Come on—I'm taking your pint-sized pekker to a specialist."

"Pint-sized? That's sixteen ounces—a full pound!"

"Pint it right this way, then," she said, bringing him to the door.

"What the—?" he cried. But she was already hauling him outside and around to his car. He didn't even have a chance to set down the tamponer.

"Drive," she said. "I'll tell you where and when."

"I'm being hijacked by a demon," he muttered. But he engaged the atomics and drove. Any time this creature wasn't interested in sex, something serious was up.

It was a party. Costumed people drifted in and out of the multiple rooms sipping glasses of wine, beer, scotch, cucumber juice, urine, and kerosene, by the smell of it. "They aren't all human," the succubus warned him privately, "so watch your language. Don't take the names of any supernatural beings in vain, or step inside any pentagrams or eat any apples or stroke any lamps. I'll see if I can find Tantamount."

"Tantamount to what?" But she was gone.

Prior drifted among strangers, nibbling a raw horseradish and sipping a horn of strong mead, alternately perching on top of the turned-off tamponer, which he didn't want to leave just anywhere. He quickly discovered that it was not exactly a costume ball. The costumes were genuine. A toothy vampire was not merely playing when he moved from woman to woman and deep-kissed each fair throat. The twin punctures remained above the jugular, though they did not seem to bother the wearers. A satyr made similar rounds, conducting the tittering victims to a separate chamber for an instant nuptial. Prior assumed at first that the vampire and satyr were fakers, but he spied blood welling out of some of those punctures and watched surreptitiously through an imperfectly closed door and discovered that the penile act was equally realistic.

He turned after that to find the vampire at his throat. "Hey!"

"Don't *do* that!" the creature said, annoyed. "You almost made me hit the carotid."

"What difference does that make? I don't want my blood sucked!"

"What *difference*! The jugular is placid, unoxygenated blood that I can keep under control. The carotid has fresh arterial blood under pulsing pressure. When my teeth dip into that, I have to seal it over hard to stop the spurt, and the toxin is carried into your system before I can recover it."

"The toxin! What are you talking about?"

"The vampire toxin, naturally. Anyone who absorbs too much of that becomes a vampire himself. Didn't you know?"

Prior backed away, holding the tamponer up as a defensive shield. "No thanks!"

"It isn't that I care about your sentiments, you understand. I just don't like the competition. Too many vamps spoil the blood."

"Just leave me alone!"

The vampire shrugged and zeroed in on another victim. The tamponer was now a liability. Somewhere along the way he had jammed into the on/off switch so that the machine was now locked on, its filament looking for an orifice to analyze. Prior set the unit on a vacant chair where he could keep an eye on it and fetched himself another drink. This one looked like rum, tasted like prunejuice, and had a kick like a shot of morphine. It would do.

"I found Tantamount," the succubus said beside him. "She'll be along in a minute."

"Who's Tantamount?" he asked again. He was watching a whis-kered man going from woman to woman and snapping their bras. It looked like fun, especially when he snapped a low-cut bra-less outfit. An excellent way of testing the firmness of the bosom, not to mention its authenticity.

"The hostess. Tantamount Emdee. I want her to have a look at you."

"MD? She's a doctor?"

"She's a penologist. An internist in penises. Uh, I wouldn't im-bibe too much of that particular brew, if you're not used to it."

"Seems OK to me. In fact I'm beginning to feel real hairy. What is it?"

"Werewolf elixir."

Prior paused to consider this. "Does this mean what I'm afraid it means?"

"That depends—"

She was interrupted by a scream. The satyr was attacking a stout woman, right in the center of the crowd. But she hadn't cried out; *he* had. The party had reached the stage where all women were willing but not all men able. She was tittering, enjoying the attention. Prior craned to get a better view. The woman had been backed up against a wall and the hooved demon was having at her. His member was mon-strous—a good foot long, about four inches thick at the base and ta-pering hornlike to a narrow apex. Prior imagined that such an instru-ment should be able to puncture panties readily and shoehorn its way into the tightest vulva—but he could not imagine any woman absorb-ing the whole of it.

Nevertheless, the satyr was the one in trouble. Frustrated by some obstruction, he had yanked up the woman's dress and underdress and petticoats and slip, and yanked down her heavy-duty panties, and was driving vainly at her corset. The thing was stoutly ribbed and crosshatched with ivory stays and reinforced with layers of canvas. Prior fancied that a cross-section of that fabric would resemble the plies of a top-grade metal-braced nylon racing tire. Stout garters and straps depended from it, serving no purpose Prior could fathom since they did not hitch to stockings, but they did effectively wall off the crotch. No wonder the satyr had been balked! The armor-like under-garment made a dandy chastity belt.

"Good evening."

Prior turned to find an absolutely beautiful woman adjacent. Her hair was a lustrous green fading to purple at the extremities. She wore an intriguing furry halter that offered tantalizing glimpses of the truly shapely breasts within. Prior studied the halter, fascinated. He was tempted to perform the bra-snap test, but there was no strap. The halter seemed to merge into her tresses without any demarcation. In fact—

In fact, her hair was the halter. It looped back from her head, parted behind, and passed forward under her arms to embrace her luscious bosom. When she nodded her head, her breasts lifted and quivered invitingly. Prior was obtaining more erectile action from those living, breathing mammaries than he had had from anything short of the slot arcade. But the sex of the slots was fundamentally dirty; this beauty was fundamentally clean.

Then he remembered the satyr. This was no sight for a lovely lady of such quality. "Let me take you away from all this," he began.

She smiled benignly. "I am Tantamount." The very consonants of the name sent charming ripples through her superstructure.

"I am incipient," he said, shifting his posture to relieve sudden and pre-emptive pressure. "Uh, Prior. Gross Prior—that is, Prior Gross."

She laughed, and her breasts did a rippling dance that nearly climaxed him involuntarily. "So I understand. Let's have a look at the subject."

"The subject?" Did she mean the satyr's frenzied attempts to get through that fortress-girdle?

Tantamount knelt before him and opened his straining fly. His penis sprang out, taut and turgid, before he quite realized what she was doing. Here in the middle of a formal party, yet! But he didn't know how to get out of this without calling even more embarrassing attention to himself. So far, most eyes remained on the Satyrical action, center-stage, fortunately.

"How large is it when erect?" she inquired, tugging at the foreskin. "Oops, beg pardon! It *is* erect, isn't it!"

Prior didn't comment. He was far too conscious of his days without a bath. The cheese would be strong, if she peeled back that prepuce any farther. He tried to back away, but he stood against a wall and could not retreat.

"The question is whether your ejaculate has particular non-reproductive properties," she said. "I had better take a sample now for laboratory analysis."

She massaged his throbbing organ. Conversation around them ceased, and people glanced curiously at what was happening. Prior would have felt more embarrassed if he had not already seen worse than this, openly performed here, and if Tantamount's touch were not so professional. Maybe the werewolf elixir had dulled his inhibitions.

She brought out a bell-necked test-tube and capped his glans with it just as he spurted. The thick white ejaculate splashed against the glass, urge after urge, until the container was a quarter full. There was a smattering of applause. Apparently the audience had expected less from so small a cock. But it was possible for a small cock to attach to a large keg.

"Very good," Tantamount said, bending to lick off a laggard smear.

The touch was so exciting to his sensitized glans that he almost urinated in her mouth. "A quite respectable quantity. Now let's check the smegma."

Prior was too bemused to stop her as she drew back the foreskin to reveal the whole purple glans. There was a coating of yellow, and the smell spread out powerfully. He stood helplessly, feeling the heat mount to his neck and face as the bystanders sniffed the air audibly.

"Excellent," Tantamount said. "I see the succubus told you not to wash it, so that a suitable specimen deposit could form."

Prior was immensely relieved. It was all right!

As his erection inexorably diminished, she took a plastic slide and scraped off a rich smear of cheese. "I'm so glad to see an uncircumcised organ," she remarked. "So many today are mutilated." Several of the men around who had begun to snicker now looked chastened. Evidently they had been mutilated, and were unable to manufacture decent samples of cheese.

"I'm convinced that smegma," Tantamount continued blithely, "despite certain charges against it, serves a necessary function. It is of course an olfactory stimulant that arouses some women." Indeed it did; most of the women in the room were breathing deeply and edging closer to Prior. "And to me the natural, complete organ is a thing of beauty—genuine masculine appeal. The esthetics are so much more important than the measurements. The male organ really should not be cut, any more than a person's tongue or nose should be cut."

"Butchery," Prior agreed. With this encouragement, both ego and penis were rallying. It was true; he did have an unmutilated member. For the first time in his life, people were contemplating his diminutive phallus with respect.

Tantamount held the cheese-encrusted slide in one hand and the test tube of ejaculate in the other. She stood up without support, lost her balance, and had to aim her pert derriere at the nearest chair, her microskirt flouncing out prettily.

Prior cried an incoherent warning, but too late. She came down firmly on the tamponer.

For a moment she perched on it, her skirt concealing the action. An indecipherable expression crossed her face, but she did not spill her samples or make an outcry. There was a click.

Then she stood up carefully and marched sedately from the room with the undisturbed specimens.

Prior put away his penis and checked the box. The counter indicated one tampon expended. He peered after Tantamount and shook his head. That was a woman worth knowing.

Chapter 7—Contest

Action elsewhere drew his attention again. The satyr had finally gotten past the barricade and into the nether bifurcation of the corseted woman. He was servicing her with the abandon of long-denial-now-abated while the onlookers clapped in unison with the thrusts. Otherwise, things were routine, considering the company.

"Did you meet Tantamount?" the succubus inquired, coming up beside him.

"I certainly did. She—took specimens."

"Of course. She's a doctor. She's probably in the laboratory right now, analyzing them. She'll get to the truth of this."

"She's quite a woman."

"That's nothing. You should see her sister, Oubliette."

"I can imagine."

"I doubt that."

The satyr finished with the corset and looked around for new romance. "Come on, banana-cock," the succubus said as she broke away from Prior. "You'll never make it with these mortal dames. Their cunts are just flesh. I'll show you how to fuck so you'll stay fucked!"

The satyr turned to meet her with a snort. "Is that so, suckbuss? You bisexuals think you know it all! You're just amateurs. Let's see you absorb *this* motherfucker!" And he brandished his impressive weapon, tall and strong despite its recent workout. A satyr was, by definition, insatiable; his member never lost its potency.

"You call that a motherfucker?" she inquired derisively. "Just call me 'Mom'!"

They went at it standing up, with the spectators gathering into a large circle. Prior watched amazed as the towerlike penis plunged into the wide-open cleft—six, eight, ten inches. She had said she could take nine in a pinch; evidently she had understated the case. "That deep enough, sister?" the satyr grunted. "I struck bottom two inches ago..."

"I don't know, brother. When are you going to put it in?"

With an outraged snort the satyr rammed home another inch, though the going was obviously difficult. The base of his member distended her cleft, seeming almost as thick as a third leg, but she didn't seem to notice. It had to be an act; she must be hurting inside, her demonic gut wrenched three inches out of line. Maybe her flesh was more elastic than mortal tissue.

"Cut out this preliminary diddle and start screwing, Granddad!" she said bravely.

The satyr battered at the connection, hammering himself in by short hard blows to his own short-tailed rear. Gradually the remainder of the ponderous member got inside. They waltzed around the floor, two figures with but a single crotch, and every spectator marveled at the authority of the connection.

The satyr started thrusting in a business way, now. Slowly the slick horn came out an inch, slowly it squeezed in again. Out in, out in—faster, now, and with a longer stroke. Prior saw the succubus' hips swell with each full insertion, spread by the mass of that trunklike base. Fluid dripped to the floor—not semen but lubricant. The tempo accelerated; the succubus' feet began to leave the floor at the height of each thrust, and her breasts were shining with sweat where they bulged out of her costume, their nipples swelling like miniature penises. "Put it to me, Goaty!" she gasped.

Then he came. He rammed so hard that she rose into the air and stayed there, hung on his phallus. She wrapped her legs around his narrow hips and hooked her feet together, riding there while he bucked his torso ferociously. Prior fancied he could see the bulge of the liquid bolus forming within the satyr, pressuring its way through an aperture that seemed all too narrow at this stage.

There was a sound like escaping steam. The succubus leaned back and threw her arms wide, so that she projected from the satyr's torso like a woman-breasted phallus. His belly appeared to collapse, hers to swell, as the bolus transferred in a series of grotesque heaves. What an emission!

Finally she leaned all the way down toward the floor, backward, her belly distended with the mass of ejaculate, and slurped off his pole. That incredible member was still hard; it sprang up again as her weight left it, glistening.

She was changing already, her breasts and hips flattening but her abdomen still bulging. "Bend over, uncle!" the incubus cried, his own penis telescoping where the hole had been.

"Here's shit in your eye!" the satyr said, presenting his hairy posterior.

The incubus wedged his instrument against the tight anus, clasping the other about the middle to gain leverage. Prior was appalled, but could not take his eyes from the show. The member would not go in. "Get your turdhole open, cousin!"

"Get your pisser hard!" the satyr replied. But slowly the orifice yielded and the eyeless head entered the first inch or two. The audience applauded.

After that initial breakthrough, the anal sphincter gave up and the rest of the incubus's well-oiled organ slammed in to its full length and depth. Properly embedded, the demon started pumping. Again the piston-strokes made the floor shudder as their velocity increased. Again the orgasm gathered itself deep in the fundament, shaped itself into a missile, built up with fire-hydrant force. The bolus tore its way back into the body of its originator, doubling the diameter of penis and anus as it charged through. Now the satyr's belly bulged as it filled. Someone made a sound, half scream and half sigh, transfixed by the sheer magnitude of this fornication, and Prior could not tell whether it was satyr, incubus or audience.

One complete round was done. But the contest was not over. Prior continued to watch with avid horror, though his shorts were sodden with his own spontaneity.

The incubus began to change without withdrawing. The transformation took care of that: in a moment the succubus stood with her vagina plastered against the satyr's anus.

He farted.

"Touché!" the vampire yelled.

Then they commenced the second round. Prior knew this one would be worse than the last, for the bolus had grown. Someone's tubing was sure to burst!

Chapter 8—Tantamount

Tantamount tapped Prior on the shoulder. "Come with me," she murmured. She was excited. One look at her heaving, hair-bound bosom was all the persuasion he required. He had had a couple of emissions recently, but his suffering penis pointed the way. He could come again—with her.

She brought him to her laboratory, to his disappointment, not to her bedroom. "The ejaculate is normal," she said, "but the smegma is extraordinary! I tried the sample on two VD cultures, and it destroyed them both. Mr. Gross, I believe you have the specific antidote to all venereal disease!"

"In my cheese?" he asked, astounded.

"Please don't be uncouth. Your smegma is phenomenal, if that tiny sample is typical. I shall have to set up a foundation to study it, to isolate the active elements, to make confirmatory analysis, to distribute worldwide—"

"My cheese?!" he repeated.

"Your smegma. This is a great moment for civilization! My name will be known wherever venereal disease abounds."

Her animation was contagious. "That's great! And I guess it explains why the cures were irregular. When I washed my penis—"

"Precisely. No penis should be washed too often, but yours especially must remain in its natural state. So I'm sure you'll want to cooperate. The last great barrier to completely satisfactory sexual intercourse shall come down, thanks to your contribution."

"Sure," he agreed, not certain what she meant. "But I can only produce so much ch—er, smegma. I can't keep trotting in here to—" Though if, by any chance, *she* were part of the deal...

"Oh, I'll analyze it and duplicate the essential ingredients in the lab and patent the formula," she said confidently. "All I need is a sufficient initial sample. Half a pound or so should do it."

"Half a pound! That would take me years!"

"Perhaps less time, if you are properly stimulated," she said. "Shall we begin?" She shrugged out of her microskirt and began to unbind her marvelous hair.

Prior could hardly believe his fortune. "You mean sexual activity speeds it up?"

"Not exactly. But what I have in mind should accomplish a similar objective." Her two fine, vibrant, heaving breasts emerged like torpedoes from the liquidly swirling green hair.

"Sign here, please."

Dazed by the living splendors before him, Prior scribbled his name on the form she presented. He would have signed a pact with the devil, at this moment of dazzlement. Presumably doctors had certain formalities to honor before letting go. Had to do with the doctor-patient relationship, no doubt. Who was he to quibble? He had never before had access to such beauty, and her compliments about his unmutilated, world-saving penis didn't detract significantly from his ardor either. How could he even have desired the succubus, who was only a demonic facsimile of what was real in Tantamount?

She cleared retorts and burners and slide specimens off a laboratory table, found a thin air mattress, inflated it from a pressure cylinder no bigger than his erect member, and settled it aboard the table. "Lie down, please," she said.

"Me?"

"You, of course."

He had somehow supposed she would do the lying. Ah, well. He climbed onto the elevated mattress. It seemed more reasonable when he saw her gaze concentrate on his midsection. She probably wanted to play with it first. Anyway, it was impossible to say no to a shape like hers.

Tantamount put her hand on his standing penis and caressed it fondly. "You are going to make my fortune," she said, and it was almost as though she were addressing the member instead of the man. "You little beauty! Trim rather than fleshy, tidy rather than ponderous. Far more efficient than some of these elephantine slabs of meat some men display." Her touch sent fabulous ripples of pleasure through him, as did her words.

"But small," he said modestly, loving it.

"Petite, but no less masculine. Good things often come in small packages, as this handsome member demonstrates." She circled the head of it with thumb and forefinger and began a gentle up and down motion. "You are just perfect, you darling! You are certainly more noteworthy than the partial members hanging from so many men." Her eyes fixed on it as though hypnotized.

"Uncircumcised," Prior agreed. He was not inclined to argue.

"Who?" she asked as though startled to find Prior still present. "Oh, yes, of course." She stroked the penis again, and it practically purred.

After a while she put her face down and lipped the tip. "Oh, I love you!" she breathed around it. Had Prior not been tapped so recently, he would have spouted right then. As it was, he felt a slow, delicious upsurge of pleasure.

"Delightful smegma," Tantamount said, running her tongue caressingly between glans and foreskin. The warm enjoyment extended down through the entire shaft and spread outward into his body. The world was tongue and penis and rapture.

She eased off before an orgasm became unavoidable, and Prior knew that she was fully aware of his state and had it under control. Doctors had some impressive talents. Then she climbed onto the table herself and bestrode him, her resilient rounded breasts hanging near his face, her parted thighs embracing his hips. But she did not settle her luscious cleft on his ready member as he anticipated. She leapfrogged gracefully up over his stomach and chest until her dainty vagina hovered over his face. It was as appealing as the rest of her. Her labia were cleanly shaved, and looked as smooth and innocent as the genitals of a gradeschool girl. Her vulva smelled of disinfectant.

"That device of yours, on the chair," she began sternly.

Uh-oh! "I can explain," he said, speaking almost into the sanitary crack. He could see her cute clitoris wiggle as his breath brushed it, and he was most anxious to have no misunderstanding develop at this point. "I was testing this machine of mine, that—well, it—I just set it on the chair after the vampire—it's called the tamponer."

"Interesting," she said coolly. "You may retrieve your tampon now."

He saw the small string of the tampon dangling like a firecracker fuse from her crevice, and was unreasonably jealous to think that it had penetrated her body before he could. He brought one hand up to grasp the cord.

She balked him with a twitch of one thigh, the play of muscles shifting one buttock and making her inner labia slide against each other momentarily. "No hands."

Oh. Well, it was a fun game. Prior hoisted his head and reached up with his teeth to clamp on the fuse. His nose nudged her clitoris and it jumped, and moisture appeared along the entire channel from clit to vulva. He finally got hold of the string and pulled down. The tampon slid out smoothly, moist but not bloody. It fell across his chin, a damp length of pseudo-cotton.

"Consume it" she said firmly. He knew she meant it because her tight little anus puckered as she spoke.

So this was her revenge for that mishap. If he wanted to get into it with more than just cotton, he would have to oblige. And he did want in—desperately. His penis would only stand for so much, before firing a warning salvo. So he tongued the soggy, half-collapsed cylinder into his mouth and began to chew. Actually, it had a certain flavor, as though mentholated.

Tantamount nodded affirmatively, then slid down his torso to lie against him, her stomach crushing his penis flat against his own belly, her luxuriant breasts pressing down warmly.

"I have been certain for years that smegma has been calamitously maligned," she said, her breath tickling his shoulder. "Nature never produces a secretion aimlessly. Like the tonsils, like the appendix, every part of the body either has or has had its function, perhaps before civilization removed us from our divine intimacy with nature."

Prior grunted amenably, his mouth still full of the sodden mass. The tampon was infernally chewy, and this discussion did not mean much to him at the moment. Not with his poor penis wedged between his breathing body and hers, on the very verge of lubricating both tummies with wriggling sperm.

"The practice of circumcision is an abomination," she continued, squirming around just enough to keep his member at tortuously rigid attention despite its confinement. "Truly, it has been defined as 'the unkindest cut'! It was conceived as a ritual mutilation, from the notion that the young man must suffer before being admitted to adult society and status. He had to pay a price in pain and blood, before indulging in the lascivious joys of fornication. Punishment before the crime! Often the same was true of the young woman—her clitoris would be amputated at puberty, in an attempt to ensure that she never received any pleasure from the reproductive act. In Judeo-Christian times the pagan ritual was continued with the claim that 'God' had decreed the act, and finally it was suggested that it was even beneficial to human health."

Prior crammed the cotton into one cheek so that he could speak. "I've heard that, but—"

She slid up, almost milking his penis by the motion, and jammed a classic pink nipple into his mouth so that he was silenced again. "True—circumcised men do have a lower incidence of cancer of the penis. But by the same token women with their breasts amputated have less cancer of the breast. You could eliminate cancer of the brain by amputating the head of every citizen."

"Mmmph!" he agreed as she thrust her breast against his face by way of emphasis.

"And some claim—falsely—that the wives of uncircumcised men have a higher incidence of cancer of the cervix, and the smegma produced by the prepuce has been charged with the crime. The fact is, it is the frequency and nature of sexual intercourse that affects the cervix-cancer rate, not the circumcision. But even were the charge true, amputation of the foreskin would be no more valid a solution than complete castration would be to prevent unwanted pregnancies. If you attempt to solve all problems by butchery, it would be reasonable to abolish all human illness and evil by decimating the species. Genocide would certainly solve—"

"Okay, okay," Prior muttered around the delightful but slightly suffocating flesh. "I'm an *un*mutilated male, remember. I'm on your side, and I'd like to be inside your—"

"But now I have the key to set the record straight," she continued, giving him a firm turn at the other breast and pressing down so that it was all he could do to breathe, let alone talk. "I shall prove that smegma—and therefore the foreskin that secretes it—has an important and continuing purpose, quite apart from olfactory stimulation. No wonder venereal disease is rampant today, when so many males are either circumcised or unconscionably clean! This will go down in the medical annals! A specific cure for the malady of our times, virtually unknown in prehistoric societies before soap and the knife rendered man's innate defense impotent."

"But how do you know," Prior gasped, almost gagging on her turgid nipple, "if VD was prehistoric, or wasn't? Maybe lots of men had it and didn't talk about it. And what about all the other unwashed uncircumcised men that have—"

She slid back down and planted a smothering kiss on him. Then, putting her hand over his mouth and stirring up the cotton inside with one finger, she said: "The twin fetishes of cleanliness and mutilation over the centuries have eliminated smegma as a viable venereal disease prevention and made its effective properties irrelevant to survival, just as modern man's propensity for shaving his face has eliminated the beard as a survival aid. Any human capability that goes unused too many generations becomes obviated. Thus it is hardly surprising that few penises retain their ancient defenses. Yours may be a unique throwback; that's why it's invaluable."

"It's valuable to *me*!" he mumbled between her fingers. Doctors had some very frustrating propensities! When was she ever going to quit talking and get down to business? He was, oddly, becoming sleepy.

Tantamount jockeyed about until her satiny cleft caressed his much-discussed foreskin, sending more waves of titillation rippling out. "And of course we have yet to come to the primary purpose of the prepuce itself. Sensitivity! The greatest concentration of nerve endings is there."

Amen! he thought, as those same nerves deluged his brain with thrust-and-spurt messages. Ready or not, here he came—any moment now. She was teasing his poor member as it had never been teased before. No wonder she was called Tantamount!

"That is why so many conservative prudes favor circumcision," she said. "Their *real* reason, not their spurious meanderings and maunderings about health and esthetics and religion and manhood. Imagine proclaiming official manhood by *un*manning the masculine member! Circumcision cuts down on the sheer, rightful pleasure of the sexual act. It—"

It seemed to him she was beginning to repeat herself. "Speaking of which—" he gasped, spitting out the masticated tampon as his member went into its climactic effort despite the strange lassitude of the rest of his body.

"Oh very well," she snapped crossly. "Have your sinful pleasure. You men are all alike."

She positioned her crotch above his own and used her hand to angle his organ in, barely in time. The first spurt smashed into the hot chamber like water from a sluice opened at flood-stage.

Prior fought to remain awake, but somehow, frustratingly, his consciousness departed along with his seminal fluid. One impulse, two, three ... it was a countdown to oblivion. "Instead of coming, I went!" he thought with despair.

And thought no more.

Chapter 9—Donation

He woke in his own apartment, his penis itching furiously. He reached down automatically to rub it, trying to remember how the past evening had finished—and found a bandage.

A bandage! Had he come down with VD after all?

He sat up groggily, yanking at the dressing. It came away with a flash of gruesome pain. For a moment he stared at his crotch uncomprehendingly.

He did not have VD. The reality was much worse.

His penis was gone—all 3.97 inches erect.

It had been amputated.

Dazed, he sat on the bed. How could such a thing have happened? He still had his testicles—but what good were they without the delivery system?

He thought back to the party. He had seen the satyr making out with the succubus. Then Tantamount had summoned him, and—

"Why, that thieving bitch!" he exclaimed, and the effort made his nonexistent penis hurt again. She hadn't been attracted to him at all, but to his penis! So she had drugged him somehow and stolen his masculine member. For the smegma she so worshipped. She had talked so long before coming to the point in order to distract him and keep him quiet until the drug put him down; only when she had been assured she had him, had she allowed him to have her.

But he had taken no drug—not since the werewolf elixir, and that was not exactly a sleeping potion. He had put nothing in his mouth except Tantamount's lovely nipples....

No! He had chewed on that tampon!

He saw it now, with an awful, betrayed clarity. She had removed the tampon after his machine had raped her with it. She must have dosed it with something, then reinserted it. That was why it had a menthol flavor. What fiendish female cunning! He had supposed it was a ritual punishment, but it had been far more sinister.

And the paper he had signed during his bemusement as she bobbled her fine breasts, her matched and matchless breasts under his nose—that document was surely a release for his penis. He must have unwittingly—but legally—donated it to the cause of venereal research. Brother!

And what was he going to do now? Storm back to Tantamount's house and cry "Look here, Miss Emdee, I demand my penis back!"? And she would show him the signed release and that would be that. When someone donated a kidney for transplant, he could not storm back after the surgery and demand it back. How could it be otherwise with a penis?

But was he to go through the rest of his life with an effeminate hole where his meat should be? What would *that* do to his love-life? He was no succubus, to convert that hole to an impressive man-sized member at will.

Prior dressed and drove to Tantamount's house. He didn't know what he was going to do, and knew it wouldn't work, but he had to try.

She opened the door promptly. 'Why hello there, Mr. Gross! So nice to see you again."

This set him back. She was absolutely ravishing despite the mundane dress and conventionally bound hair. Now her tresses were ordinary brown—had the color been a trick of the night lighting?—and her bosom was demurely de-emphasized under a laboratory smock, and her fair face was innocent of any sign of any thought touching on anatomical matters between the shoulders and the knees. Yet he felt his absent penis stiffening, hoist by its own imagination, and he could think of nothing appropriate to say.

"Do come in," she said, as though he were an old friend. And when he was in: "Are you in pain? Let me check the dressing." She kneeled before him, opened his fly and ran her slender fingers over his smarting crotch. "Oh, you removed the bandage. That won't do. This will heal nicely, but it has to be protected for the first few days. The operation was a success." Sure, he thought laconically. The operation was a success, but the penis died. "I—"

"You were so generous, contributing to science and health this way. Let me show you."

She took him to a small office where she rebandaged him, leaving a pipette for urination, then led him back to the laboratory.

His penis was ensconced within a maze of glass tubing. Colored fluids traveled to its base, and there was the steady hum of a pump. A plaque set in the base of the display said: DONATED IN THE INTEREST OF THE WELFARE OF MAN—PRIAPUS GROSS.

Good god! What kind of a monster would he seem if he took it back now? Yet—

"You see, we have it transplanted into a compatible environment. Other organs have been kept living and functioning for years in the laboratory, such as chicken hearts, but this must be the first time it has been done with a penis. Isn't it a beauty?"

"But it's *my*—"

"And this way it will produce smegma under controlled conditions. We shall surely unlock the secret of its chemistry. Venereal disease will become a hobgoblin of the past. Between this and the Pill, there will be a new era of sexual freedom." She paused, then added with less enthusiasm: "For those who really want that sort of thing. To me it is more of a technological challenge."

Remembering the night past, he appreciated her limited candor. She was much stronger on clinical sex and lecturing than on actual man-woman performance with human feeling. She probably would not have played up to him at all if she had not wanted his penis so badly.

"But what about *me*?" Prior cried at last. "I need it too. And not just for the cheese!"

This time she didn't even flinch at his use of the vernacular. "Oh, didn't I tell you? My sister Oubliette specializes in the practical aspect. She's a bit liberal for my taste, but quite competent. She will provide you with a prosthetic free of charge, because of your service to Science. You will be very well off, by your definitions—her members are world-famous. In fact," she added with a frown, "you will be able to perform as never before."

"I perform perfectly well with my own prick, when not drugged!" he protested.

"Here is her address. She'll be expecting you." Tantamount presented him with a card.

"But I don't *want* a fake pe—"

He was already outside again, and the door was closing. She had managed him as readily as if he were a rebellious child. Perhaps he was, compared with her cynical subtlety.

But her sister Oubliette was too liberal for her taste.

Well, why not? He could stop over this evening, after work.

Prior looked at the card. The address was about two thousand miles away.

Part 2:

Prosthesis

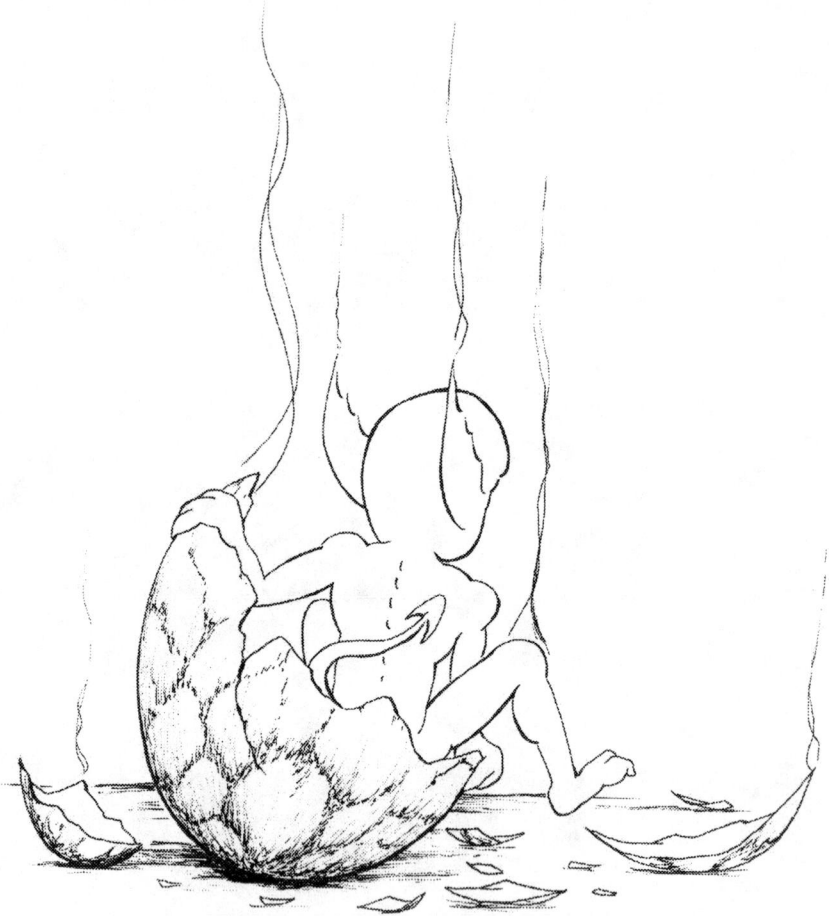

Chapter 10—Oubliette

Oubliette Emdee was, if anything, even more physically attractive than her sister. She knew the hair-halter trick, too, and filled her tinted tresses just as generously. She welcomed him warmly with a delicious kiss on the mouth. "We'll do the exploratory surgery this afternoon," she said cheerfully.

The kiss palled. "Exploratory surgery! All I came for was a fake—"

"After all, we can't very well stick it on with glue," she pointed out, taking his hand and using it to comb through her hair where it stretched across her fine cleavage. "We have to match cell types to be sure there is no problem of tissue rejection, and we have to phase in the nerves and conduits. Otherwise sensation will be imperfect."

"Sensation!" he exclaimed, in his surprise grabbing hold of her left nipple and getting a nice dose of sensation himself. "On a *prosthesis*?"

"Certainly. Ours are very special members. Every aspect must conform precisely to the original so that no one can tell that the organ is not genuine. Didn't Tantamount tell you?"

"She's more conservative about such details. I thought it would be, er, a dead stick. Like a peg-leg or imitation arm. I—uh, does that include anti-VD smegma?"

"That no, unfortunately. We can't duplicate chemical secretions from the organ itself. But everything else, yes. And you yourself should not be able to tell the prosthetic from your original while it is actually in use."

Prior pondered that. As far back as he could remember, he had been called "Dinky" or "Pinky" or "No Show" or some such, and he was of average height. Girls had turned him down, not because the size of his member bothered them, but because the ridicule associated with it did. Three point nine-seven inches erect, and less when flaccid—it might as well have been an albatross tied around his neck. "Does it have to be identical?"

"It doesn't have to be. But normally—"

"Could it be ... larger?"

"It can be elephantine, if that's what you really want. Or minuscule. Or pretzel-shaped. One man had the measurements of his horse duplicated for—"

"And will it still work just like the real one?"

"Better than a real one, because stronger and more durable."

This was beginning to sound quite promising. "I'm not sure exactly what kind I'd like. Do you have samples?"

"Right this way." She removed his hand from her tress-formed décolletage and shook that breast back into place.

Prior followed her, admiring the flounce of her hips as she walked. His two-thousand mile journey seemed worth it already.

She had a trophy room full of mounted penises. Long, short, thick, thin, human, animal, erect, flaccid—every imaginable variant. Prior was frankly amazed. "I can't choose between them. I'd like to have a big, strong one—but that seems like being unfaithful to my original."

"That's why most people duplicate their originals," she pointed out.

"But I don't like my original. That is, I like it fine, but it could use a couple more inches. I've heard of brides running screaming from the honeymoon suite on their wedding night; with me, she'd be laughing. Or crying."

"Some women prefer a compact organ."

"They may prefer it, but they don't respect it. Just once, I'd like to have a woman gasp and cringe when she saw what was coming. Instead of asking me when I expect to reach puberty. But aside from that, I'd be most comfortable with my own."

"Hm," she said, considering. "Tantamount informs me that you donated your original member voluntarily in a splendid act of magnanimity for the welfare of mankind. I presume that means she drugged you and snatched it on a technicality."

"You understand her pretty well," he said ruefully.

"Yes. So I'm inclined to do a bit more for you than I ordinarily undertake. It's a matter of family pride." She considered some more. "This is more complicated, but I could install a standardized socket. With that you could alternate members at will. Maintenance would be more critical, and you'd be in danger of short-circuit if you used it under water—"

"Short circuit! I want a penis, not a soldering iron!"

"Oh, it's not electrical—though some men do seem to want soldering irons, for what reason I hesitate to imagine. But neural connections—you could find yourself with a urine-stimulus in mid-orgasm, or vice versa. Could be awkward."

"Guess I'll stay away from underwater intercourse, then, unless she's a whore." But Prior felt a bit uneasy.

Oubliette smiled. "*All* women are to some extent—"

"You're saying I could plug in a big penis one time, and a small one next time? And they'd both work? And the doll wouldn't know?"

"I wouldn't recommend using different units on the same girl, if you really wish to keep the matter private. Women are not completely obtuse about such matters."

"Uh, yeah," he said, remembering that he was talking to one. "Sounds worth a try, I guess."

"There will be a wait of several days after the initial operation," she said as though the issue had never been in doubt. "There may be some discomfort. You'll need diversion, and erotic play won't be feasible right at that time. Do you read?"

"Last book I read was Huck Finn, in high school, and I didn't understand it."

She frowned, and the expression reminded him so much of Tantamount that he felt nervous again. Then her mouth quirked.

"Well, English teachers don't understand the introductory note on that one, either. Like sex, it is not supposed to be understood, but to be enjoyed." She made a little shrug of polite implied apology. "I have other patients, so you can't stay here the whole time, particularly if you have nothing to occupy you. I don't think it would be wise for you to go into town, either, during your convalescence. Sometimes there are complications—bleeding, spontaneous emissions, that sort of thing."

"I'll just have to suffer through," he said bravely, thinking of a rigid six-inch member projecting from his trousers in proud display. He wouldn't mind suffering some of that embarrassment! But he felt an ugly twinge in his crotch. There was many a slip twixt the cock and the strip.

"Maybe you can visit the Egglayers," she said. He didn't ask what she meant; it sounded like a chicken outfit.

Chapter 11—Socket

Prior went under the knife on schedule. Oubliette laid him out on an operating table, strapped him down, focused a spotlight on his groin, and swabbed him off. Then she stripped to her working clothes: sandals and that hair-halter. Prior developed a splendid nonexistent erection.

"I don't like being encumbered when I operate on a man," she explained. "The scalpel might slip, and right now I have no assistant to mop up."

He eyed her magnificent torso and agreed that this was a hazard to be avoided. He wondered why she had no assistant. Was it because a male helper would be too distracted by the doctor's uniform to take proper care of the patient, while a female would be too skittish about the specific anatomy being handled? Or were Oubliette's methods too proprietary to permit possible competition? Or did she just like to do things her own way...

She put a mask over his face.

Prior dreamed he was a satyr with a permanent thirteen-inch erection. He was looking for a woman to spread out for an innocent hour of febrile fornication, but something was wrong with each candidate. The first was so fat that he couldn't find the hole; it was lost amidst the folds of flab. "Fuck it, you eunuch!" she kept screaming. "You have three minutes! Two minutes! One minute! Thirty seconds! VIOLATION! Serves you right, slow-poke!" The second was shapely but small; she screamed when only three inches got inside, and when he rammed in six she split open like a smashed melon and lay on the bed in two bloody halves. The third was very good; but when he sank in eight inches there was a loud CLICK and something started to whir inside her pubic cavity. His member began to hurt as though being hacked apart, or perhaps being peeled like an onion, but it penetrated another inch, and another. Then he realized: she was a pencil-sharpener, and she was grinding his pencil down to the nub. He tried to pull out, but he was locked in. It was worse than Korea, Viet Nam, and the following similar wars: the more he strained, the more he lost.

When he woke, there was indeed pain. He felt as though a curling iron had been rammed into his gut and left at low heat. For the first time in his life he regretted being male. Surely this was a hell of a lot of trouble for a little tube of erectile tissue. Then Oubliette entered the recovery room, still garbed in her working clothes, and he decided that it was after all worth it. Oh to have a member to penetrate that tantalizing cleft! The sooner the better. The bigger the better.

"I have a heavy schedule," she announced. "Two emergency cases just got in—a harem Sultan had his organ stepped on by an irate camel, and a homosexual just discovered that his natural penis is allergic to both saliva and fecal matter. So—"

"How could a camel step on—"

"Some are more sensitive about bestiality than others," she said. "I warned him about that last year. Stick to horses, Sulty, I told him, and female ones, because they're less ornery. But he wouldn't listen. Had to find out the hard way. Now I'm sending you off to visit the Egglayers for a few days. When you come back, you'll have healed over and I'll have matched the tissue cultures and we'll be ready for the next stage."

"Uh, sure," he agreed dubiously.

Chapter 12—Statues

So it was that Prior Gross, bearing a plaster cast at his crotch with an embarrassing spigot for urination, departed for a land he had never known existed. Behind Oubliette's spacious modern house was a pathway leading into a tangle of virgin scrub. Along this anemic scenic highway were unusual objects of art—statues of people, animals, and things. At the end of it, she had assured him hurriedly as she swabbed a local anesthetic on the Sultan's mangled meat, were the Egglayers.

"What do I want with a bunch of chickens?" he demanded, disgruntled. But she only smiled enigmatically and eased a plastic catheter up the Sultan's urethra. The bloody urine was just beginning to squirt as Prior got out of there.

He rode on an adapted golf-cart. The trail was too narrow for his car, and his cast prevented him from walking any distance without severe chafing, so this awkward compromise was best. He puttered along at ten miles an hour. It was an electric cart, but still it puttered.

The first statue was a nude woman. She was, of course, statuesque in outline. Oubliette herself could have been the model: the breasts were round and full and bursting with the milk of human sex-appeal; the waist was tiny, and the hips swelled with exactly the right planes and rondures. The breasts had realistic nipples, the tummy had a navel, and between the legs there was even a cleft complete with clitoris and vagina, the last as deep as his finger could probe. He had verified this purely as a matter of scientific curiosity, of course.

Why should such a finely-wrought piece of art be erected at this deserted outpost? The trail was virtually unused; grass grew tall between the weathered concrete sections and flowers peeped from chinks.

Yet this nude was good enough to take to bed, stone though her hole might be.

Prior shook his head and drove on. The world was full of pieces of art that should have been pieces of ass.

A mile along he discovered a similar edifice, this one supporting a male. Handsome, muscular—very much in the classic Greek discus-thrower mode, except that this one's hand cupped not a discus but his ponderous turgid penis and full scrotum. Though the member was enviably large, it was also well-shaped and not disproportionate to the physique of the statue. It was an embodiment of the ideal in just the fashion the rest of the man was. And, Prior noted with satisfaction, it was uncircumcised.

All penises were beautiful, he thought, before the knife practiced its mutilation and left ugly scar tissue choking an obscenely naked glans bereft of the body's most sensitive nerve endings. Tantamount had been right about that. No wonder the penis was now the most concealed part of the human body. Women's breasts were beautiful, their genitals inviting, because they represented completely natural secondary and primary sexual characteristics. But the average person, male or female, averted his/her eyes in unvoiced disgust at the sight of penis and bag of testicles. Was this merely a natural aversion to overt disfigurement?

And what about the emotional disfigurement that seemed to follow in the wake of the physical? How much more readily a man with an ugly penis projected that ugliness to sex itself! Was it not true that beauty was in the penis of the beholder?

The next statue was of a sheep—a fine curly specimen good for at least three bags of wool for master, dame and boy down the lane. The fourth one was a dog, a tremendous Great Dane sitting on his haunches and reaching around to lick off his partially-extruded penis. Dogs, Prior remembered, really did have a bone in their members. How many human beings wished for the same! Then on along to spy a horse, and an eagle, and then a griffin. Followed by a combination: man and sheep.

Prior stopped to inspect that one more closely. He had been right the first time: a male man and a female sheep, and the connection was more intimate than one normally observed on the farm. The ewe stood upon a platform so that her woolly posterior came up level with the man's crotch. He stood behind her, his hardened member half-buried in her ovine pudendum and still thrusting. She looked tolerant and contented. Prior remembered that there was a story about interfertility of man and sheep, a crossbreed between the two ... but he doubted the validity of that. "Ba-a-a-a!" he commented.

Next were a male dog and a female human in much the same situation. She was on hands and knees, he mounted behind, tongue hanging out in his enthusiasm. Her breasts drooped toward the ground, almost tubular in this position. It was so realistic that it was hard to believe that it was all stone. Stone it was, though. Those swinging mammaries were cold and hard to his touch; the furry flank quite stiff. Even the projecting tongue was dry and inflexible, and there was absolutely no warmth or give to the plunging prick.

Then there was a male pony having at a female eagle. At first glance this seemed a mismatch—but Prior soon saw that the pony had no real leverage, so that his member could penetrate only as far as the bird desired. There seemed to be plenty of desire amid the feathers, however.

And a trio: man, woman, griffin. The griffin was in the center, spreading its huge wings, beak open as if to caw exuberantly. It appeared to be hermaphroditic, for its leonine penis was entering the woman who clasped it in front, while the man drove at its womb from behind. Its long tiger tail curled around the man's buttocks, holding them steady.

It occurred to Prior that he had not seen a single portrayal of a really unnatural activity along this trail. Always a normal male conjugated with a normal female in the normal manner. No homosexual efforts, no perversions. Of course the species were shuffled—but the acts depicted by the statues were so obviously right and pleasurable that he could hardly fault them on a technicality like that. Sex between consenting adults was perfectly legitimate. Wasn't it?

Then he spied a representation of a man with his baby. The man's penis was flaccid; but even more remarkable, he had a well-developed bosom, and the baby was nursing.

Prior stood and stared at that for some time, his groin twinging nervously. Was this a sculptural joke? He had never heard of a man with full-blown breasts, except for the chosen castrates who claimed to have converted to women. Yet every man did have nipples, and before puberty the chests of boys and girls were pretty much alike, and in some cases boy-babies dribbled milk from those nipples. So the potential was there—and if man was not intended by nature to have it, why was he born with nipples? Only body chemistry in adolescence made the difference. Why not men with breasts and women with beards?

Could it, in fact, have been this way in the past? Less differentiation between the sexes? Perhaps at one time every adult human being had had beard and breasts, and penis and vagina. Maybe only in historic times, when prudery could be developed, perfected and spread like a vile disease, had the woman's member been reduced to the clitoris and the man's hole portioned between anus and urethra. Once man had fought his way to supremacy on Earth, he had no longer needed to have every part interchangeable, and so true sexuality had developed. A modern woman could be considered at least in part a castrated male; a modern man might be a debreasted female.

Prior shook his head, embarrassed by the turn his speculations had taken. Next thing, he would be wondering whether there had originally been any differentiation between man and sheep and horse and bird and griffin. The statues implied that there had not been; that all could revel together sexually; that evolution had altered only the forms, not the sexuality.

Well, maybe so—but what kind of offspring would spring from the merged loins of man and griffin? The heraldic beast was already a cross between an eagle and a lion. Even the man-sheep combination was complex enough; would that be a mashep? Sheepan? Meep? Shan?

He paused. Maybe a succubus, or—

Satyr.

Satyr! Of course! Forepart of a man, hindpart of a goat. Bipedal, but with horns. No doubt it all made sense, once the big picture was viewed and grasped.

There was a good deal to learn from such statues. Maybe someday he would return for the whole course of instruction.

Chapter 13—Eggers

At last he arrived at the outpost of the Egglayers. At this point Prior was ready for anything. But his buildup was only for a let-down.

It was a small conservative cabin. The road looped around it and stopped. There was nowhere else to go.

He marched up and knocked on the door. After a moment a middle-aged saggy-gutted balding man yanked it open. "This is the place," the inhabitant said abruptly, his whiskers quivering like those of some cartoon character. "I don't recognize you, though. Mighty small gut on you. You new?"

"I guess so," Prior admitted. "I was told to look for the Egglayers."

The man reassessed him, scratching his ponderous belly. "You ain't an Egger?"

"I guess not."

"Then whatinhell you doing here?" the man roared.

"I don't exactly know. I'm supposed to stay here for a few days until ..." He trailed off, not wanting to be too specific.

The man let fly a sigh as though breaking wind. "Well, come in anyway. Maybe we can train you."

Prior entered. The interior was every bit as humble as the exterior had promised. There were cobwebs in the upper corners and roach droppings in the lower corners. But he was hungry and tired and his crotch hurt and he wasn't looking for trouble or for palatial accommodations. He wasn't much for mystery, either; if the man cared to explain what the Egglayers were, fine; if not, who cared?

There was bread on the dirty table—a monstrous brown loaf, partially sliced. Beside it was a frothy bucket of brew. Prior helped himself and eased into the chair. Almost with the first bite he felt the gases bubbling in his intestine; this was flatulent stuff. "Who told you about the Eggers?" the man demanded as though just thinking of it.

"Oubliette Emdee. You see, she—"

"Oubie! Whyinhell didn't you say so?" The man belched resoundingly, and a faint putrid vapor drifted from his mouth. "Anything that li'l pekkermender wants is just fine with us!"

"She told me to come here for a while so my preliminary operation can heal. Because she has other patients, and it gets crowded."

"She's busy, all right. But she's got plenty of space. Must've wanted you here ... sure you didn't come to learn Egging?"

"I don't know anything about—"

"You'll find out!" He laughed with unseemly gusto. "Who's she got under the knife this time?"

"A sultan had his member damaged by a—"

"That camel-humping African? Haw, haw! He never learns! She must've warned him fifty times: stay clear of the camels, Sult; one fuck too many and they fuck you back. Specially the he-camels. But that old shitter, he—"

"And a homosexual with allergies to saliva and fecal matter."

"A fairy what don't like spit or shit on his horn! Cheese, Oubie really gets the cases! How's your maypole sliced?"

"I don't understand—"

"You don't see Oubie just 'cause your swinger don't stand, you know."

"Oh. I was deprived of my member, so she—"

The man crammed a slice of black bread into his big mouth. "Hmd y'oos yr motherfucking coch?"

"Beg pardon?"

"Who sawdoff yr stinkin' horseradish?"

Somehow the question didn't sound much better the second time around. Maybe it was the mouthful of food that made it sound messier than it was. "I was rolled," Prior said with simple dignity.

Black crumbs spewed violently out of the man's hairy mouth. "Prick-rolled? My bellowing asshole! You don't say! Ain't that a jock-popper!" And he chuckled roundly.

It seemed best to get this mirthful loudmouth onto something more productive. "Do you know anything about prosthetic members?"

"Dead stick sledders? Never tried it myself, but I hear Oubie's the best fuckin' cocklock in the business."

"You mean there's no sensation in the prosthetics? She implied—"

"You're farting through your yellow teeth, junior. Sensation? When Oubie sews 'em on, just pissing can jack up your bug juice."

"Especially underwater, I understand." But Prior took this as a favorable report. "What do you do here, really?"

"We lay the eggs." He pronounced it with a long e. "Didn't she tell you?"

"Not in sufficient detail."

The man perked up a hairy ear. "Clucker's comin' now. You just watch."

Sure enough, another magnificently bloat-bellied man barged in. "Well if it ain't Plymouth Rock!" the newcomer cried. "But who's yer mistress?"

"Oubie's threadin' his clapper to the rucksack," Plymouth explained. "What's your load, toad?"

"Gimme the nest, pest," Clucker responded.

Plymouth brought out a box filled with straw. It did look like a nest.

Clucker touched his soiled buckle and dropped his filthy trousers and shorts. He squatted over the nest, his huge meaty buttocks spreading impressively.

"Watch," Plymouth directed, pressing Prior's face down almost into contact with the straining brown-streaked rectum. "Now you'll see some real chickenshit!"

The hairy pink anus bulged. Gas leaked out, as though an old-fashioned bus were starting, and the aperture fluttered shut. Prior gagged from the stench, but couldn't get his head away. Then the flesh bowed again. It turned outward, blue veins showed, and the central cavity deepened. Something white appeared in the ugly depths.

A white turd? Prior marveled. Did the man have a liver-bile blockage? He had heard that bile was what made fecal matter possess its normal rich brown. When the bile duct got constipated, the stuff backed up in the liver and had to run through the blood, finally making the urine brown instead.

The pale lump pushed out. It was rounded and smooth, and its surface glistened. On an oily film it eased out of the heaving bowel. It was about the size and shape of a hen's egg.

An egg! Something halfway registered in Prior's mind. They did call themselves egglayers!

The egg dropped into the nest. Plymouth picked it up and studied it closely. "Good shape, good heft, Clucker. You sure can hold 'em."

"Incubate it," Clucker grunted. "Sometimes the end one gets cold."

Plymouth carried it carefully to a glassed-in nest and set it inside. Clucker strained over his own receptacle again. As Prior watched, another egg emerged. This too was incubated. Then a third and a fourth.

Clucker stood up and hitched aloft his trousers.

"You go to all that trouble just to carry a few eggs?" Prior inquired.

"Eegs," Clucker said. "E-E-G."

"They look like plain old chicken eggs to me."

"Takes some chicken to lay an eeg," Clucker said amiably.

"The first time, that is," Plymouth said. "Our layings don't count;

that's just transport."

"I don't understand. Why don't you just carry them in a basket, or a regular box of a dozen?"

Plymouth burst into laughter, his belly shaking St. Nick fashion. "Shitfaced inspector'd just love that start, fart!"

"Also, it's cold on the pass," Clucker said. He finished his mug of brew, burped, hauled the nest around and dropped his pants again.

More slowly now, and with increasing grease, two more eggs passed. Then, after a labored pause of several minutes, a couple of chunks of odoriferous fecal matter and a seventh egg.

"You longtongued cuntlicker!" Plymouth exclaimed with admiration. "You packed an extra!"

"Going to shit for the record one of these trips," Clucker said, pleased.

"You sure got a voluminous intestine! Five's the best I can manage. I'm afraid of breakage. What if I took a jumpstep on the pass and they knocked together?"

"Occupational hazard," Clucker said, wincing. "I thought sure I'd cracked one, once, but I guess I hadn't, 'cause here I am today."

"But what's the point of it?" Prior demanded. "Cramming eggs into your ass?"

"Who the fuck is this turd?" Clucker inquired politely.

"Oubie sent him along. Says he got pekker-rolled."

"Oh—another dope who'd lose his cock every time if it wasn't screwed on! And it wasn't, eh?" He laughed unkindly. "But I s'pose if *she* speaks for him, must be hokay." He turned to Prior. "Hokay, you wanna know what's the fit, shit, I'll tell you. We pick' em up on Beetlejuice VII and smuggle' em past customs and take 'em through the pass. There's a fence here on Earth who retails 'em for the standard markup or more. Layers like us make good loot, long's we're careful. I figure to retire next year, if I don't bust an egg goin' for the record."

"Good money?" This always interested Prior.

"Thirteen seventy-five per eeg viable," Clucker said. "Makes ninety-six twenty-five this trip, my cut."

"Cut-cut-cut-daCU-U-UT!" Plymouth put in, sounding so perfectly like a cackling hen that Prior had to laugh. But he remained amazed.

"Almost fourteen dollars for an egg?"

"Thirteen hundred and seventy five dollars, sterling," Clucker said curtly. "Eegs ain't cheap."

Prior couldn't digest this figure, so he didn't try. "Where'd you say they came from?"

"Beetlejuice VII. You know, seventh habitable planet of Betelgeuse, the red giant. Long trip."

"I guess so. Just how far away is it? I thought the stars were several million miles."

"Several hundred quintillion miles," Clucker corrected him. "Give or take a decimal."

"Uh, sure." Prior regretted having made the inquiry.

"'Bout 650 light years," Plymouth said helpfully. "Be 'un 'ell of a trip if we didn't use the pass."

"'Ell of a trip," Prior echoed. He still didn't understand what was going on. "I didn't know we had space travel. From star to star, faster than light, I mean."

"I told you. We use the pass. Cuts it way down."

"You told me," Prior agreed. Some things he just wasn't fated to grasp.

"Any more due this week?" Clucker inquired.

"Rhose Island Red tomorrow. That's all on the schedule, until the fence comes next week."

"Rhose Island Red, huh? Red's a good fuck. I like her."

Until that last word, Prior had not been certain of the sex of Red.

"Yeah," Plymouth agreed. "'Cept for the way she slips an extra eeg up her front hole."

"Whatsamatter with that? If I had a woman-hole, I'd use it too. Cop the record for sure!"

"Stretches her honeypot all outa shape. Got to wait a good hour 'fore it's tight. Anything I hate, it's a loose woman. 'How's the hunt, cunt?' I asks her, and she says 'Take yer pick, prick.' Then she's too loose for me to get a good lodging. And even after a day or so, she still ain't exactly in Oubie's league."

Prior perked up. "You Eggers have intercourse with Oubliette?"

"Huh?" Two blank stares.

"You know. Cohabitation."

Plymouth squinted at him suspiciously. "You a Communist?"

"Sex!" Prior yelled. "Did you ever screw her?"

"Whyinhell didn't you say so! Sure we fucked her. Never got to the bottom of that well, though; deepest dame you ever fingered."

"Course usually she's too busy," Clucker admitted. "So we leave her be unless she comes out here. Which she does, every month or so. Great gal!"

"Sometimes she hardly gets by the statues," Plymouth said, inspecting the last two eegs. "All tuckered and fuckered out, can't screw mor'n three-four times before she nods off, and once or twice after that."

"She spends time looking at the statues?" Did she find them as dismayingly fascinating as he had?

"Yeah, and they look at her!" Both men laughed crudely. Prior didn't get the point of the joke, so he ignored it.

"Hey, Cluck!" Plymouth called suddenly. "Listen here."

"What's the word, turd?"

"I think it's bad luck, fuck."

Cluck joined him at the incubator-nests. "Great flying shit and little blivets on the halfshell!" he cried. "One of 'em's pippin'!"

"That's night hatching!"

Clucker listened more carefully. "Not yet. The pips are still pretty far apart. Might be two days 'fore the shell breaks."

"But the fence ain't comin' for five days!"

"Thirteen seventy-five down the shittin' tube!" Clucker moaned. "*We* sure can't fence it." They paced the floor gloomily. "That damned ET!" Clucker exclaimed. "Looked me up the nose with all three eye-balls and swore on his kingfeather those eegs were fresh! I'll piss a river down his windpipe!"

"That ET don't *have* a windpipe," Plymouth reminded him.

"He'll have a couple when I get through with him! It ain't just the cash. What if it'd hatched up my ass?"

"It's stuff like that makes me think 'bout retirin' early."

"Early hatch—that's retirin' the hard way!"

They paced some more, in obvious distress. "Say," Plymouth said. "Oubie always wanted an eeg. You think—?"

"Hey, that's a real birdbrained notion!" From the tone, that was a compliment. "We owe her a lot. We'll give it to her!"

"Except neither one of us can take the chance of going to her place. If we got caught in realtime—"

"Fartin' cunts!" Clucker exclaimed, chagrined. "I forgot. She'll have to come here for it."

"Might not be time. If we miscalculated—"

"Yeah. Can't risk it. Not with *her*."

Then they both looked at Prior, struck by a common thought. "He's going back there anyway, and he's mundane," Plymouth said. "No timespace barrier."

"Sure, I can carry an egg to Oubliette," Prior said agreeably. He was glad for the pretext to get away from these odd, gutty, lowbrow, foulmouthed, foulassed, indecipherable men.

"Good enough," Clucker said, visibly relieved. "First thing in the mornin', we'll load you up and send you back. Be a real nice surprise for her."

Only as he drifted to sleep in the midst of a surprisingly comfortable bed of straw did Prior begin to wonder why, if it were so chancy for Oubliette to carry her eeg back before it was hatched, it should be safe for him to do so. Was it because no one cared if he met calamity?

Chapter 14—Enema

One detail they had neglected to mention. The eeg, in a delicate condition, had to be maintained at body temperature, kept in darkness, and insulated against all severe jostles. It could not be transported in any external basket.

Well, they knew how to handle that. Plymouth Rock held Prior down while Clucker pried apart his tensed buttocks and greased his rectum with a horny finger. Then Clucker dipped the eeg in tallow and then in slippery oil, and applied the narrow end to Prior's pursed sphincter. "Open up," he complained. "We got to slide it in without cracking."

"It *hurts*!" Prior protested, objecting on more than one level to the violation of his anus. "My operation—"

"Can't be helped. Just think of it as shittin' backwards. This ain't fairy stuff, now; this is an eeg." He rapped on Prior's lower spine with a calloused knuckle. Prior jumped—and in the moment his sphincter loosened, the eeg slurped in.

"Easy as bittin' a balky horse," Clucker said, satisfied.

"Work it around in there so it's comfortable," Plymouth remarked. "You don't want it down too close to the asshole, case you sit down hard or pop it out with a fart. Up around the curve of the gut is better."

"Um," Prior said, making swallowing motions with his anal canal. "What happens if it hatches early?"

"You got a morbid sense of humor," Clucker said, unsmiling. Prior decided not to pursue that matter farther, since the eeg was already lodged.

He departed on his puttery golf-cart, feeling the mass of the eeg in his bowel. What a profession!

The roadside statues remained. He could have sworn that some of them had changed their positions. If he ever came this way again, he would make exact notes and discover whether the various scenes of copulation were in fact in slow-motion progress. But right now the weight he carried and the ominous warning of the Eggers reduced his inclination to tarry along the way.

He made it without trouble. "Back already?" Oubliette inquired. She didn't seem crowded or busy—but who was he to question her? Maybe she had simply felt he needed the kind of education provided by the Eggers.

"I brought you an egg. Eeg."

"An eeg!" she gasped. "Prior—you didn't steal it?"

"I'm no thief. More'n I can say for some people," he said, thinking of Tantamount and his bygone penis. "Clucker and Plymouth Rock sent it to you as a gift. It's pipping."

"Oh!" Hastily she brought a nest. "Lay it before it hatches! You're too young and innocent to die like that."

What shook him was the fact that she was perfectly serious. Prior squatted over the box and strained, not really caring that she was watching. She'd seen his crotch before—hell, she'd operated on it.

The eeg, funneled well up his large intestine, refused to come down on demand. Oubliette poked her finger well up his tract but couldn't reach it, though the act did start a throb in him that would have been a hard-on in other circumstances.

"We can't wait," she said, alarmed, and he believed her. She brought a tube and inserted it into his rectum, driving it deep. He wondered whether this was what a woman felt like during intercourse, as the male member probed her vestibule. Then the warm bubbly water gushed into his colon, bloating him, and he wondered again. The sensation wasn't half bad, actually. She must have put something into the enema-rinse to relax his innards.

She brought a metal potty and aimed him at it. "Push it all out," she said urgently. "I'll catch the eeg."

Prior strained. A jet of pale brown water shot out, splashing against her fingers. She had her hand right there, caging his anus, to make sure the eeg didn't slip by her and shatter in the pot.

Prior pushed and pushed, and the water squirted down end-lessly, filling the pot and splashing Oubliette's hand, arm, bosom and face, but the eeg didn't come. Finally he trickled to a halt, unsuccess-fully drained.

Well, not entirely unsuccessfully, he noted as he examined the container. There were several mangled chunks of fecal matter that had evidently been caught and sifted through her fingers along with the fluid. The smell was about normal for the situation.

"It's too far back," she said. "We have to get it out quickly. I may have to operate."

Prior looked at her brown-stained hands and arms. He didn't like the sound of that. "It's up here somewhere," he said, touching his abdomen.

"Let me see." She threw back his shirt and probed his belly, feeling for the solid egg. "Yes, here it is! Maybe I can work it down."

She pressed and pulled at his gut, squeezing at the object within it. Prior contented himself with studying her flexing cleavage as her arms worked. If he had a penis, she'd be almost in position to suck it now, he thought wryly.

"I have it down some, but not enough," she said. "Maybe I could reach it with forceps—"

"Another enema might carry it down, now," he suggested quickly. He certainly could do without hard metal forceps wrenching around within the tender folds of his intestine.

"Well—perhaps a thorough one," she decided. "But if this doesn't do it—"

"It will do it!" he said prayerfully.

She fetched a longer, larger tube and about twice as much water as before. "Lie back—I want this all in there without leakage."

Prior lay on his back, knees lifted, while she screwed him again with the spurting tube. This water was cool, and it pumped in interminably, chilling him from the inside out. This time he didn't just feel bloated, he *was* bloated; he could see the bulge of his abdomen, and knew that his insides were being shoved around by the ruthless torrent of water. As the bodies of succubus and satyr had been distended by their exchanged bolus of ejaculate. Just so long as none of his piping sprung a leak.

It became urgent that he squirt it out again, but she used her knees to press his buttocks together and seal off the leakage around the outside of the hose. She kept pouring in more water, holding the feeder-tube as high in the air as she could to increase the pressure. It felt as though there were three gallons inside him already, yet still it came, distending every conduit available within his torso. Now it was more than bloat; it was agony.

"Close it up!" she said at last, hauling out the hose and ramming his legs tightly together. His sphincter barely cooperated; the dike was about to burst. "I'm going to maneuver the eeg down while the water lends support."

Prior struggled and sweated and finally managed to constrict his protesting anus so that only a trickle of fluid emerged, though his whole urge was to let fly. He had never labored so hard at anything in his life before; the cold liquid seemed like a solid battering ram as it hammered at that puckered portal with every breath he took. Part of the urgency was sexual—except that now the desire to fuck was as nothing compared to the plain need to shit!

Oubliette probed his gut again, kneading his belly, and Prior almost blasted a liquid round from his rectum. She worked the eeg around and down; he could feel its sloshy progress as the hydraulic pressure translated directly to his anus.

"It'll come now!" he gasped. "It'll come. Let me at that pot before I explode!"

Slimy fluid was already dribbling down his legs as he got into position. "Ready?" he panted.

"Ready," she said, squatting behind him and cupping both hands under his tense nether orifice.

He let fly. Water blasted against her hands and sprayed across the room in a steady torrent. It was like letting the air out of a balloon: he deflated visibly as he pressed that column of water out. He imagined that there was a phallus attached to his anus, and this was the world's champion ejaculation, coming and coming ... and he felt a genuine orgasm coming on.

The pot filled and overflowed, but still he jetted. Then the flow diminished, hesitated; his imaginary penis grew climactically hard, and—

In a spurt of yellow juice and a transcendent orgasm he laid it: a sparkling, rapidly-pipping ovoid. Oubliette caught it with a little shriek of delight and held it gingerly. "Whew!" she sighed rapturously as the fury of Prior's anal climax abated.

There was more water to shit, but the impelling need to evacuate was gone. He slacked off like a spent thunderstorm and stood up, shaking his dripping legs. He looked at her.

Oubliette was spattered from eyelash to toenail with pale brown or yellow dye. Her clothing was dripping, and a marble-sized turd was lodged in the cleavage of her hair-halter. She stank of shit, but she was oblivious to that. She held the eeg-egg close, cooing at it while fecal fluid dripped from her pert nose and made her lush breasts glisten.

It seemed she appreciated the gift of the Eggers.

But they had labored prematurely, however effectively. It was a good ten hours before the eeg hatched, and by that time Prior was back under the knife.

Chapter 15—Eeg

He woke. This time he found solidity at his crotch. Not a penis—
a base structure, part flesh and part plastic. The region around it
hurt, of course, but he took this as a sign that the nerves were still
functioning. Nerves that could bring as much pleasure as pain, when
the occasion presented. To this ugly sub-structure would attach the
penis proper—and he hoped fervently that it would perform as specified. It had, he thought with a half-bitter internal smile, been a real
pain in the ass to get this far.

"One more procedure will do it," Oubliette announced briskly,
looking amazingly clean and chaste and smelling the same. She was a
marvel! One would think shit had never come within a mile of her
person. "Come see my little eeg."

She already had a special enclosure for it. The eeg/egg had indeed hatched, and in the warm nursery toddled the eegling. It looked
a little like a griffin and a little like a goblin, but more like a walking
phallus with priapism: a perpetual erection.

"I don't see any mouth under that beak," Prior remarked. "How
does it eat?"

"It's demonic," she explained. "It doesn't eat."

"Well then, how's it going to grow? I mean—"

"That's a hell-lamp," she said, gesturing to what looked like a
complex sun-lamp. "The radiation gives it all the energy it needs. Demons are creatures of hellfire, pretty much."

"I guess so." He shook his head dubiously. "What does it do,
when it grows up?" He was glad the thing hadn't hatched in his colon,
for it had snaggle-teeth (despite the absence of a mouth) and wickedly
hooked beak and saber claws and spiked tail and barbed wings. Not

to consider its supremely massive (proportionately) phallus.

"It fornicates," she said.

Ask a silly question...

The next operation was minor. In fact it was not an operation at all, but a series of intricate tests. Oubliette connected his stub to a computer input and manipulated dials and settings and made what he presumed were significant readings. Sometimes he felt twinges in his crotch, sometimes irritation, and finally a testicle-bursting smash of erotic convulsion.

"Tests out well," she announced as he stopped thrusting. "We'll give it another day to set, then we'll run it through some practice exercises."

Prior was getting tired of surgery and testing. "When do I get my penis?"

She merely smiled obliquely and went to attend to her next client. He had to satisfy himself with watching the eegling sporting in its enclosure. Oubliette had given the thing a bit of Swiss cheese, and instead of eating it the eegling rammed its comparatively monstrous member into the holes and sawed away with indefatigable vigor. It never ejaculated, but of course it was only a couple of days old. Prior imagined that there would be copious ejaculate by the time it attained its full growth—and if it became man-sized, its phallus would be about two feet long. But he didn't see what there was about the ugly little demon that was worth over a thousand dollars for shipping charges alone.

Chapter 16—Practice

The practical exercises, when they came, were well worth the wait. Oubliette opened a sealed package and lifted out a limber three-inch artificial penis. Three short stiff prongs emerged from its base. She aligned it and plugged it into his genital socket. "You lock it on this way," she said, giving it a twist and snap. "Reverse the motion to remove it. You'll get the hang of it with practice."

"I don't feel anything," Prior complained, eyeing the dangle. Had he gone through all this, just to wind up with a member even smaller than his original?

"This unit is factory fresh. It hasn't been activated. Here." She ran her finger under its glans.

There was a pop! and sensation coursed into his groin. The organ quivered.

"Now to test it," she said matter-of-factly.

She began to manipulate the organ by hand, paying special attention to its sensitive tip. Prior felt the stimulus, but the member remained flaccid. She put her lips to the glans. Still no physical reaction, though the sensation was enough to make cooked macaroni stand stiff.

"Something's wrong," she said, brow furrowing attractively. She wrenched the organ about, giving Prior a shock of agony. Then the lock released and the penis came loose.

Oubliette inspected it closely. "No wonder! The artery profunda penis is blocked. You couldn't pump any blood into the erectile tissue. Darned sloppy quality control at the penis plant these days."

"You mean the thing can't get stiff?" he asked, disappointed.

"It will stiffen after I adjust it, or I'll have its head," she said confidently. She reamed it with an instrument resembling a pipe cleaner. "Remember, when you change members ordinarily, do it in the flaccid state. Otherwise you'll lose blood, and it could be messy and embarrassing."

"The valve cutoff doesn't work?"

"No trouble there. But in the erect state the member is engorged with your blood. If you remove it before that fluid reenters your body—"

"Oh." He saw the problem. "Why would anyone want to remove an erect penis?"

"Sometimes there are emergencies. Or a client changes his mind during a performance."

"Hm." The possibilities were intriguing.

She reconnected the reamed member, locked it, and resumed stimulation. This time it swelled magnificently in her hand. At full elevation it had doubled its limp state: six inches long and perfectly formed.

Prior stared at it, bemused. He had never had a strapping lout like that between his legs before. It was like winning a sexual sweepstakes.

"Well, the proof of the pudenda," Oubliette murmured approvingly. She dropped her skirt.

Yes, indeed! Prior was suddenly so excited that he skipped the amenities. He bent her back over the work table and thrust his capacious member at her sweet cleft. It bounced off harmlessly. "Oops-forgot to allow for those two extra inches," he said, not particularly displeased. It reminded him of those bygone ads about the extra long cigarette and all the attendant disadvantages. Cigarettes, of course, were phallic representations; that was why so many people got hooked on sucking them, and liked them long and strong. Two extra inches were well worth some inconvenience.

Oubliette just smiled tolerantly. Obviously she had been through this sort of fumbling before.

Prior oriented more carefully and found the slot. As his big handsome glans nudged into her shaven slit he felt the pulsing warmth of her. He worked the tip of the member inside, finding the channel moist and slick, savoring every aspect. He was going to do big things with this big cock! He was really going to go to town! This clever female doctor was going to get a proper workout!

And as he forced the sensitive first inch into her luxurious and educated vagina—he came.

"Damn!" he wailed, but it was too late. The pump had started, and it would not desist until the entire cow had been milked, the pipe cleared. His angle was wrong, so that he could not penetrate more than that inch while the cream spurted. What an opportunity wasted!

"Slight over-sensitivity there," Oubliette commented professionally, applying absorbent tissue as the member dropped away. "I'll detune it for you."

"No-no, I like it that way!" he protested despite his chagrin. "I'll get used to it. I always shoot off early when I haven't had a—when I haven't done this for a while."

"As you wish," she said with a suggestion of medical disapproval. "This unit seems to be fully functional, in other respects, and the foundation seems adequate. But we should try a reasonable selection."

She twisted the flaccid member so that it snapped off. Some blood dripped from its base, giving him a shock until he realized that even a detumescent organ would have some stuffing in it, particularly after use. At least the automatic seal on the base structure was functioning; nothing leaked from his body. There was evidently some very nice technology involved.

Oubliette washed off the unit at the tap, shook it dry, wrapped it in gauze and replaced it in its box. "These should be cleaned regularly, of course," she said. "And boiled in a salt solution once a week if used regularly. The prosthetic is never quite as convenient as nature's original."

That was an inconvenience he would gladly accept. Despite the prematurity of his ejaculation, the experience had been memorable. Six inches erect! It was like a wrestling championship, a bowling award, a grand prize in anything—and look whom he had wrestled with, look what he had bowled over!

She opened another box. "Now this is one of our most popular numbers," she murmured in sales-clerk tones as she broke the seal. She hauled forth a four-inch dangle and attached it. "Try it erect."

"But I just—I mean, twice in a row? I never—"

She removed her hair-halter and showed her fine bosom unadorned.

Prior's new penis climbed invisible stairs. At the upper deck it stood: a proud eight inches, slender but strong. He looked down at it amazed and fundamentally gratified. This doubled his best natural erection. He felt lightheaded; could all the blood have gone into the member, lowering his blood pressure elsewhere? A trifling inconvenience!

"Sometimes a substitution of units restores potency quite promptly," Oubliette remarked casually.

"I think your breasts had more to do with it."

"Oh? They're prosthetic, of course."

"Prosthetic!" His erection wavered and threatened to collapse.

"My little joke," she said quickly. "I grew these naturally. See for yourself."

He saw for himself, with hands and eyes. His hard-on became mighty indeed.

"But it really shouldn't make any difference," she said with medical detachment. "Your prosthetic penis is as serviceable and esthetic as the natural one, and prosthetic breasts would be the same. I have a professional friend, Bovinia, who specializes in such procedure."

"Women want larger breasts?" he inquired, intrigued.

"Many do. But her main business is replacing injured mammaries—ones that have been beaten or bitten beyond repair—"

"Beaten or bitten! What sadist would do a thing like that?"

"Not necessarily sadism. Merely overly enthusiastic love-play. And some are lost through cancer, even today. Then of course she has a fair trade in the gay community."

"Men? Men with breasts?" Suddenly he remembered the last statue on the route to the Egglayers.

"Certainly. Bovinia and I exchange referrals. When a couple wants to change over, I take care of the penis for her, and Bovinia handles the mammaries for him."

"And they actually work?"

"Well the ejaculate isn't potent and the breasts can't be used for actual nursing, but apart from that—"

"Yeah" he said, dazed. If the other doctor's breasts were as good as Oubliette's penises, no client should have a complaint.

Yet it didn't seem the same. His prosthetic member was big and handsome and potent, but it wasn't *him*.

"We might be more comfortable on the bed," she hinted.

They were. A cubicle adjacent to the laboratory had a firm bunk offset by large wall-mounted mirrors. It was ideal.

Prior spread her out on her back and lifted her long lithe legs so that her cleft parted. He kneeled appropriately and wrestled his member down to nuzzle the dark opening. This time the angle was correct, and the curved head pressed between the pink lips and slid inside without obstruction. He watched in the mirror as the long shaft disappeared: two inches, three, four. Probably his own previous ejaculation provided the lubrication, for this was almost too easy.

His legs felt cramped, and he had to pause in place to straighten them out. He braced his arms against her thighs, keeping her legs elevated, and leaned into his chore. Another inch entered, and another.

The Eggers had been correct about Oubliette being bottomless. Six inches deep, and he hadn't met resistance yet. Seven. Finally his loins met hers, pubic bone grinding against pubic bone, and the mirrors were useless. That was the trouble with mirrors, as with pictures—a complete entry showed nothing. Cartoons always showed the cock half-cocked, with only a couple inches submerged, so that it was quite clear that fornication was occurring, but who in real life ever stopped there? (Except for the dolt who climaxed at that stage; he could think of one of those, alas.) If he wanted a picture, maybe some kind of X-ray photography, that showed a solid penis ... no, the X-rays would pass through the penis too; it just didn't seem feasible. Only

Superman had X-ray vision that showed things X-rays did not, because Superman was a fantasy. Sex, unless carefully posed, was inherently private, for purely physical reasons. Unfortunately.

Meanwhile he had a situation here. Oubliette had absorbed all
his eight inches without complaint. What good was it to double his
phallic size, if he still couldn't touch bottom? Also, his first performance, truncated as it had been, slowed this one down considerably.
He wasn't close to coming.

Then her interior muscles began to operate. She squeezed his
organ, kneaded it, milked it without laying a hand on it. Prior had
never experienced the like. Peristaltic ripples traveled up and down
her slick canal. Pressure, suction, pressure, suction, squeeze and draw
and stroke—and before he knew it he was spewing his essence with
an imperative abandon he had never experienced before. It did not
seem to be dulled because it was the second; rather it seemed to reach
farther into the roots of him, extracting pleasure from hitherto un-
tapped springs.

She let him subside inside her, and that was another kind of
bliss. "Yes, I'd say the operation was a success. No doubt your technique will improve with practice."

Prior didn't answer. He had thought he had done a bang-up job,
but evidently he operated in a lesser league. Oubliette must have been
screwed by experts.

"Now," she said briskly, "for the next exercise—"

"You're joking! I never came twice that soon in my life before. The
orange has been squeezed dry."

But she had little patience with excuses. "This one is special. It's
prehensile."

"Come again?"

"You will, you will. And this time I will too, and we can call it a
night. Wouldn't want to overdo it for your first workout, after all."

"No..." he mumbled agreeably.

She affixed the member. It was S-shaped, about eight inches long
even when flaccid, but no thicker than a pencil. It looked unnatural
on him, and he didn't trust it.

"Let's have an erection," Oubliette said crisply. "This will require
a little practice, but you'll find it is worth it."

"I'm spent," he said regretfully.

"You have not yet begun to spend. Do you think I went to all this
trouble just to have you poop out for the main event? Now let's get this
crate into the air."

Prior tried valiantly, but the crate only twitched and hung its
snakelike head.

"This is insubordination," she said, irritated. "I'll goose it into
action." She brought out a douche-shaped vibrator. "Bottoms up."

She had not been speaking metaphorically. Prior turned around,

leaned over, and presented his posterior to her. She turned on the
vibrator and pressed its horn into his quivering rectum. He was getting goosed by a professional. For a man who did not like pederasty,
he realized his anus was getting a lot of attention. First the Eggers,
then the enemas, and now this.

But the treatment was effective. His twisted organ jerked. It was
as though the nerves of his colon connected directly to his penis. Maybe
they did, now; how could he know the details of the surgery he had
had? The S-shape began to straighten out, and the pencil-diameter
swelled into fat crayon size.

Oubliette put more pressure on the vibrator. It nudged deeper
into his anus, tugging at the membrane, one inch, two. It dilated the
sphincter muscle and gave it a royal rubdown. It stirred up his bowel,
sending a pleasurable and somewhat urgent warmth outward through
his entire diaphragm. And the phallus expanded.

He felt the vibrator sliding yet further in. It reminded him of the
enema tube, but this was three times as effective for arousal. *This*
must be what it felt like for the woman, as the man's hard member
thrust into her inch by inch. When his pulsing glans throbbed up
against her cervix, did she feel—

The tip of the vibrator struck something. It added a new dimen-
sion of sensation. It was as though he were already ejaculating—but
he wasn't. A phantom yet pleasant orgasm.

"Prostate," she murmured.

Whatever it was, his erection was now complete. Some ten inches
of serpentine penis bobbled under his belly. This one had not doubled
in size; it had a different structure.

She withdrew the vibrator. It felt as though he were defecating,
but it remained a most satisfying experience. His anus closed about
the retreating horn as though to hold it in, but there was no holding it
as it popped out. He straightened up and turned to face her, the organ
waving like a slender tree before him.

"Now you control it by employing particular synapses," she said.
"The muscular structure is built in; there is no direct tendon contact,
of course. But once you get the trick—"

Prior tried, but the long thin phallus merely shuddered into a
slight reminder of its limp S format.

"I think we can prompt control," she said. She brought out a
shining hypodermic with a cruelly long needle.

"Now wait a minute!" Prior cried nervously, backing away.

"It only hurts for the first five minutes," she said reassuringly as
she aimed the needle at his glans. "After that it settles down to a dull
ache. Try not to scream; it might disturb the other patients."

Prior's buttocks spread against the cold wall, halting his retreat.
"Can't we do it some other way?"

"This is fastest." She put her left hand against the wall to stop him from sliding along it. She reoriented the hypodermic spike in her right. "Now the first shot goes in the base of the glans, under the foreskin. Hold still, because the needle has to penetrate almost half an inch to reach the main nerve, before the spider venom is injected—"

The penis whipped to the side, away from the threatening needle. "Spider venom!"

"Yes, that's how," she said, taking the needle away. "Some organs respond more readily to threats than to promises."

Prior was shaking. "You mean you weren't really going to—?"

"Not unless your tool failed to perform," she said a bit smugly.

"What's *in* that pigsticker?"

"Sterile water. But of course I wouldn't puncture a prosthetic, since it can't heal."

Prior was still breathing rapidly. This doll was deadly!

At her direction, he learned to wiggle the penis from side to side, to hook the tip around, and to make an undulating S shape. The motions were clumsy, but he could see that with more practice he would be able to put this member through an impressive array of tricks—in or out of a vagina.

"Now let's harness it," she said. She got on her hands and knees on the bed and presented him with a hole-shaped orifice. This was about the only position, he knew, where the hole really was a hole—when the weight of the body was pulling away from it, allowing air to enter and spread it wide. He wondered whether he could see down to the end of it, if he had a penlight.

But this was no time to dally. Prior kneeled behind her and formed his member into a crude corkscrew. He concentrated on her crack and lunged his penis forward like a striking snake.

He was not as proficient as he thought. The serpent caromed off one resilient buttock and sprawled ignominiously against her leg. He hoisted it again, no-hands, and drove for the center crevice. This time it was on target horizontally but not zeroed in vertically, and it came up against the puckered clean anus. He shrugged and applied torque; she'd been into *his* ass more than once, after all.

But the resistance was too great, and his control too fumbling. The glans snapped out and skidded down to the waiting vulva, where it sank in easily.

Prior gave it a ripple and watched the slender length of it tunnel in. Air escaped as the mass of his entry displaced it from her open vagina. Down, down he drilled, undulating against the hot walls of her channel. Three, four, five, six inches. He felt the mouth of her cervix, and angled the glans to stroke it repeatedly. He wondered whether it would be possible, with this unique organ, actually to penetrate the uterus itself. No, probably not—not without damaging the womb. That region was reserved for sperms and babies and intra-uterine contraceptive devices.

Oubliette sighed, and he knew he was accomplishing something. But he was determined to plumb the full depth of her this time. In he went, a greased piston. Around the cervix, beyond it, down into the very nadir of her cavity. Seven, eight, nine inches.

Then at last he felt it: that cushiony resistance that signified the end of the alley. He straightened out the python and wriggled in the last inch, thrashing the head back and forth rapidly. He was going to stir up her gut the way she had stirred his!

"Oh," she moaned. Her breathing accelerated.

Prior leaned against her cool derriere—so unlike her blazing interior!—and reached both hands around and under to titillate her hanging breasts. That was why they were called tits, he thought: for titillation. These were fine and full, their nipples erect. He took one in each hand, hefting it as though weighing choice meat, and corkscrewed simultaneously with his embedded penis. He caught each nipple between thumb and forefinger and rolled it back and forth while his glans chafed at the dent in her cervix.

She groaned and struggled and flexed her bottom against him, and her breath escaped with a slight whistle, but still she did not climax. Prior, despite his two preceding efforts, was close to making it again. But he was determined this time to take her with him.

He had an inspiration. He let go one breast and moved his fingers to the front of her cleft, reaching around her thigh to come at it squarely. He dipped his forefinger in the lubricant of her two parted inner labia and rubbed back until his finger struck his own buried shaft, then forward again to her clitoris. Then he pinched the clitoris and mashed it up and down several times.

Now at last her buttocks grew hot too. Her back arched, her body stiffened, and she panted. He hooked the tip of his finger into the little fold of the clit and squeezed it back into its base while he shoved Prehensile with all his might.

Oubliette climaxed explosively. He had punched the right button this time! Her hips bucked back into him, her breasts flopped against each other and her buttocks tensed convulsively against his loin, squeezing his organ from its base all the way in. She jerked back and forth, riding his shaft, pumping herself along so that naked inches showed momentarily, only to be swallowed up again. Her entire vulva tightened around him, the labia closing on the base of his member, and inside that peristalsis wrung him in waves and tidal waves, concentrating much of his blood and all of his sensation within her.

Prior came. He had to.

It was like spitting into a hurricane. He knew he was spurting, but he couldn't feel it amid the violence of her motions. Then she screamed and sighed and shoved back against him so hard it hurt, and her vagina clamped as though she had turned to metal or stone, and his last throb pressured out deep inside her with slow, agonizing, hydraulic force.

She collapsed forward on the bed, and he with her, still connected at breast and hole. Her bottom bunched and became softly
rounded, cupped enticingly under and against his loin, and as she
relaxed outwardly and inwardly his penis slowly softened within that
liquid mass of flesh. He was panting right along with her, and still
kneading the breast that was now flattened against his palm. It was an
utterly delicious sensation.

After a time he rolled off her so she could breathe. He thought he
had lost erection entirely and fallen out, but he had forgotten how
lengthy this member remained in the flaccid state. A good four inches
of semi-turgid flesh pulled out of the hot shadow between her nether
mounds.

"You're coming along nicely," she murmured into the pillow. "I
think one day you'll make a skilled lover. Tomorrow we'll try some of
the more advanced exercises."

Chapter 17—Pigskin

In the daytime Oubliette had her regular patients—a steady stream of men with damaged, undernourished, or impotent penises. Prior didn't inquire into their specific complaints. Obviously they did not have the privilege of playing the music of their organs for the pleasure of the doctor. He was a special patient, and he knew when he was well off, and he intended to stay out of mischief to be sure the situation didn't change for the worse. But daytime was dull.

He wandered through the library. Idly he took down a volume and riffled through its pages: *Psychopathia Sexualis*, by one Krafft-Ebing. Just as he had suspected: dull as hell. He glanced randomly at the spines of other volumes: first editions of *Chin P'ing Mei, Bah-Numeh, Exeter Book, Complete Letters of Marcus Argentarius*, and so on: all exotic, dated, obscure references of no conceivable interest to him. Not a good sex novel in the bunch.

He contemplated the pictures on the wall, but they were oddities of classical vein—Aubrey Beardsley originals, the erotic art of Pompeii, and similar. There was some decorative statuary—INDIAN EROTIC SCULPTURE, the plaque said. He yawned, not inspecting the stuff closely. Too bad Oubliette's literary and artistic tastes weren't the same as her medical ones.

For want of anything better to do, he visited the eegling. Its play-pen was under a map of the United States, the nation somehow looking like underpants stretched across North America with the penis that was Florida poking out to spray the urine that was Cuba and the Antilles. Some pale splotches suggested that the eegling had been using the map for phallic target practice, and now had something in its member to squirt with. But for the moment the creature ignored the map and eyed Prior mischievously.

The eegling was larger already, especially its standing member. It strode up to Prior's side of the pen and jetted a drop of thick fluid at him. There was a faint whiff of butterscotch.

"Fuck you," Prior told it irritably. "To me you're no better than shit, and I'm the one who shit you."

Prior drifted back to his room and lay down. His crotch itched, so he opened a drawer and took out the largest of the attachable units and plugged it in. He lay on his back and watched it come alive. It took time to fill, for it had voluminous capacity. It would be disastrous to remove this one in the erect state: not only would the job be messy, his body would be deprived of a fair donation of blood.

And that would be an interesting way to donate, he thought as the tube of prosthetic flesh lengthened and thickened against his belly. Plug in a transfusion bag instead of a penis, then show stag films. Maybe the nurses could be nude. Maybe they could give a man a real thank you for his donation. Put on a huge prosthetic, ram it into luscious nurse, take it off immediately after climax so she could pour the blood into her pot. In five minutes the average man might pump a painless pint out through his crotch, trying to fill a donation organ. Whoever received that blood in transfusion might feel horny as hell, too. If a pretty young woman needed blood, they could set up the input inside her vagina, and have a mating mechanism on the penis: his erectile blood goes directly into her body ... Little old lady in tennis shoes waking up and saying to the male attendant "I think I need a transfusion; gimme a quick fuck before the doctor gives me my sleeping pill"...

Prompted by his chain of thought, the member stood complete at last: twelve inches long erect, two inches thick through the massive glans. Prior could not even circle it with thumb and forefinger. What a monster!

It was a circumcised model. He didn't like this feature, but was morbidly fascinated. He licked his finger and ran it over the nude purple glans. There was sensation, but not as intense as that available from a foreskinned member. He wondered how men with such mutilated organs ever managed to ejaculate. Maybe they just had to try harder.

Curious, he wrapped a section of bedspread around the thing and tugged it snug. It wasn't exactly the same as a living, pulsing vagina, but it represented enclosure of a sort. He clasped both hands about it and pressed down.

Now the gargantuan phallus responded. It throbbed against the confining cloth like the motor of a powerful car, swelling to even greater magnitude. He had been wrong about circumcision; it was possible to get adequate stimulation without the foreskin. He pumped the wrapping a couple more times, feeling the urgency develop. Ah, where was

Oubliette now!

The door banged open. A grandmotherly woman bounced in and collapsed upon the easy chair across from the bed. "I'm so glad to find a waiting room that isn't crowded!" she exclaimed. "All those dirty old men..."

Prior glanced anxiously at his lap. A section of bedspread stood like a tower before him, a foot high. He couldn't put the thing away without unwrapping it—even if he cared to remove it erect—and he couldn't unwrap it in front of this unwanted visitor. The absent-minded or near-sighted grandmother had somehow mistaken his bedroom for a waiting room.

"What's in the package?" she inquired sociably. "It almost looks alive."

"Oh, it's the living end," he assured her weakly. "Are you sure you have the right room?"

"I'm not sure of anything since poor Herbie came down with cancer of the cock," she said. "He used to be a good fuck, but now he can't even get a good hard-on. A soft-on, is all. I have to use a banana on my cunt before I can get to sleep."

Prior stared at her, disbelieving what he had heard. She still looked every inch the conservative retired housewife. "Herbie has cancer? That's too bad. Must slow him down."

"Slow him down? Hell," she said crossly. "My grandson can fuck better than Herbie now, and he's only eleven. I sure hope the doc can patch up that prick."

"I hope so," Prior agreed. The monster within the bedspread showed no inclination to lie down.

"What did you say was in that package of yours? Smells familiar."

"Nothing of consequence," he said quickly. "Just a hunk of meat."

"Herbie loves meat," she said. "Makes him potent. Now he won't touch his regular food. I've become quite a connoisseur. What kind of a cut is it?"

"Choice."

"Are you sure? You know the state laws are very vague about grades of meat these days. Butcher will slip in an average cut and charge you for prime."

"I'm sure this is satisfactory." Prior found himself sweating, but his member refused to shrink.

"Just the same, I think I'd better have a look at it," she said in the way grandmothers have with young men. "I wouldn't want you to get cheated." She stood up and approached, not to be gainsaid.

"I haven't been cheated!"

But she was already pouncing on the package. Prior sighed and let her unwrap it. It might do this busybody good to get a shock like this.

She peered at the monster, squinting. "You're right," she said after a pause. "That's choice."

Prior rewrapped the meat, afraid to inquire whether she had recognized what she had seen.

"I haven't glimpsed such a fine cut of first-class boar pizzle in years," she said. "It looks almost alive."

Ah, so. "Actually, it's synthetic."

"Oh, no, it's genuine. I assure you, I know my meats." Prior decided not to argue. Grandmothers could be very certain of themselves, particularly when they were short of information.

Meanwhile, his erection maintained itself in full splendor, though he felt no slightest sexual inclination at the moment. There were, he could now appreciate, certain disadvantages to twelve inches.

"Mrs. Cobblestone," a PA down the hall announced. "Please collect your dog."

"Oh goody, Herbie's ready!" she exclaimed, getting up again.

"Herbie's a *dog*?"

"You know how it is. He thinks he's people. Oh, I hope his poor little cock doesn't hurt too much!" She bustled out.

Prior shrugged. Alone, he unwrapped his meat and contemplated it. Boar pizzle indeed!

Finally the thing subsided and he removed it. In the future he would be more careful what penis he wore when and where. His four incher had never really embarrassed him in public; his concern about untimely erections had been vastly exaggerated. Now, with the availability of the ultimate twelve-inch wish-fulfillment, his concern was genuine. He would not again unlimber that cannon unless he intended to fire it.

He spotted some small lettering on the base as he washed the unit out. He squinted to read the fine print.

It said: 100% PIGSKIN, Grade A Choice.

Grandma had been right.

Chapter 18—Graduation

"Tonight, the advanced exercises," Prior said, smiling with anticipation.

Oubliette shrugged out of her clothing. "Precisely. I've had a busy day. Have you ever tried to operate on the penis of a cancerous toy poodle?"

That would be Herbie. "Never had that pleasure."

"Fortunately it was a false alarm; the growth turned out to be benign, and I was able to save his member by skin grafting. Animals don't do well on artificial genitals; they don't understand them. But what a job!"

But surely worth it for Grandma Cobblestone, who would otherwise be dependent on her eleven year old grandson, or on bananas. To each his own lifestyle.

She fetched a box. "Now this is the Pipecleaner model. Useful for the tight vagina. I'm afraid mine won't do for demonstration purposes, not even with a stiff dose of alum, so you'll have to practice on the anus." She affixed the unit.

Prior peered down at it. The thing looked like a strand of spaghetti swishing loosely over his scrotum.

"Erect it," she said, lying prone and spreading her slim smooth legs. The sight of that perfect behind and the shaped shadows within it did the job immediately. His spaghetti advanced from cooked limpness to dry brittleness. It had been well named: it did resemble an old fashioned pipe-cleaner, one of the narrow furry ones that children delighted to use for making stick-figure animals.

He climbed on, bracing himself with elbows and knees. He lowered the member. It brushed across a prettily dimpled buttock but would not orient properly on the crevice.

"No hands," she cautioned him. "At least, not there. You have to learn how to maneuver it alone."

Prior grunted and shifted, and finally the thin tip scraped down to the deepest shadow between the cushiony creases of her derriere. He pushed—and it slid off below. He tried again, but this time made entry the easy way, in her vulva. At last he centered on her sealed little anus and drilled it down. But it was dry, and he penetrated only with difficulty and pain.

Prior withdrew, moistened the slightly odorous tip and column with saliva, and finally forced it in a couple of inches. The thing was so thin he was afraid it would break off. But once he navigated the sphincter he was all right; the remainder cruised deep into her warm bowel, and the sensation wasn't bad at all. The exercise wasn't really so difficult.

"Now try it on a moving target," she said. "Out."

He withdrew it reluctantly, as he had been thinking of jetting soon. Oubliette began bouncing her generous buttocks about. They rippled and quivered as though made of gelatin, fascinating him.

"In," she ordered.

He tried, but couldn't get a line on the jiggling pucker. Every time he got close, it moved, giving him at best a miss and at worst a painful dent in his slender implement. "But what's the point of this?" he cried, exasperated.

"Some day you may have to get into a ticklish virgin," she said. "Or it might be necessary to rape someone. I never want it said that you left my office unprepared."

What was she training him for—the war between men and women? This was more like hand-to-hand combat than love play. Certainly he never figured to drill any of his new members into any unwilling recipients.

Little did he know.

He finally zeroed in on the gyrating target and injected the hypodermic. But before he could climax, she stopped him again. "You've caught on to the technique. Now we'll try the triple fork."

"Triple fuck?"

"Triple *fork*. Once you master that, you're there."

"I'll settle for a good honest penis."

She disengaged, to his regret, and trotted across the room for another box. He watched her buttocks bunch and crinkle as she went. What he could do with the twelve-incher now!

The box was huge. Two feet long ... impossible! No penis could be that size in the flaccid state— not if it expected to find lodging within a human pelvis. Even a horse would be hurting!

Horse? He remembered the Sultan and his camel. Oh, no! Surely Oubliette didn't mean to make him attempt that.

The reality was even more amazing. It was not one penis, but three. Rather, one divided into three. The longest portion was indeed two feet; the others, couched like testicles at its base, were of normal proportion. But how could such an unbalanced tripod ever be used?

"This design dates from medieval days," she said, holding it aloft with a certain pride. "Devils used to employ it during black masses and such, but now the patent has passed into the common domain. It takes a really virile man to apply it successfully."

"*Three* rods?" Prior feared he wasn't man enough even to figure it out.

"Put it on. You'll see."

He put it on. The long shaft had a bone in it, so that it was always erect and needed no infusion of blood; the other two were flaccid. The weight of the trio yanked cruelly at his loin, reminding him that his socket had not yet healed completely.

Oubliette got on her hands and knees again and presented her handsome posterior. "Stations, men," she said.

Seeing her there, Prior finally realized what this weird divided member was for. The two small penises lifted as his hot blood filled them.

He came at her as he had the prior night, but with a difference. He had three members to insert. The long one passed between her legs and curved by her falling breasts to reach her mouth. The two lesser ones prodded simultaneously at her vagina and anus. It was tricky getting them aligned, but with patience and steady nerves he made it.

He concentrated first on the rectum, wetting down that penis and ramming it home until the sphincter yielded. Once he had that entry, the vaginal one was easy, though he did have to bend it around by hand so as not to withdraw the other. It would have been easier had they been in line instead of side-by-side—but he realized that then other positions wouldn't be feasible. No sense specializing into non-versatility. And the mouth-organ was already in place.

Vaginal, anal and oral—simultaneously. Those medieval devils had really known how to fornicate!

But he wasn't home safe yet. He was receiving sensation from all three extremities, and it confused him. Oubliette was sucking on the mouth-organ and clenching her sphincter on the anus-organ and performing her patented peristalsis on the center pipe organ. It was an organ symphony! He could have enjoyed any of the three melodies individually, but in concert they were too much. It was like juggling balls while walking a tightrope blindfolded—and his balls had been triply depleted the evening before. He did not know, literally, whether he was coming or going.

This was, indeed, an advanced exercise.

He tried to coordinate his thrusts, but the mouth-piece went astray while the anus-entry jammed. He pulled back, and both mouth and vagina disconnected. The anus clung to its member, compressing the glans. That one was about ready to fire. But would it be good form to spurt in one place and not the other two? Was it, in fact, *possible*? They all connected to the same fundament, after all.

Prior was sweating.

If the medieval devils had come naturally equipped—assuming that an unnatural creature could be said to have natural endowments— with such tri-part penises, they must have had a hell of a time forni- cating. Maybe that was what it meant to be damned.

He thought he heard Oubliette chuckling.

Damn it, he was *not* going to fail this test! She thought he couldn't do it, that he wasn't man enough to handle a super-phallus like this. Once a four-incher, always a four-incher, she thought. Well, he would prove that he was a two-footer!

He juggled the swinging mouthpiece into place again. He angled the six-inch, thick-bodied member back into her slippery vagina. He plunged the third, thin cock all the way into her rectum. "Fuck you!" he cried.

"Fuck me!" she echoed, still amused.

Why was she so light-hearted about it? After all, she was con- cerned too; she was the one getting the business end. She acted as though she were only a spectator.

Spectator...

Maybe that was his mistake. He had been concentrating on his own management, forgetting that sex was a two-person action. He couldn't have a climax without taking her with him; that would be just half a copulation. There had to be *inter*action; she had to come too.

He found that with the proper contortions he could leave the anal penetrator anchored while he slid the other slowly in and out of her vulva and held the two-footer in place except for some sidewise vibration. This served to equalize the stimulation, letting the sphinc- ter-bound member cool off while the others heated. He was getting the hang of it.

He commenced a balanced offensive on three fronts: (1) Into her mouth, where her tongue lapped around the slender instrument, send- ing two-foot waves of pleasure back to his loin and, he trusted, into her throat as well; (2) Into her anus, where the tight sphincter muscle contrasted to the roomy interior, stirring up her bowel in what ought to be a provocative manner; (3) Into her luscious vagina, haven of deep delight, rubbing at the sensitive cervix to make her respond.

He no longer needed his hands for support. He reached around her midriff on either side and caught her breasts, massaging the nipples until they sprang out vigorously. He pressed them together around the shaft of the long member, squeezing it evenly. It was impressive for him, feeling his thrust through enveloping mammaries, but for her too, for breasts were made to be caressed.

Oubliette was breathing hard now, responding to the triple on-slaught. She caught the long penis gently with her teeth, nipping it as her breath caressed its hollow tip. Her buttocks pushed back against his crotch, absorbing as much of the nether shaft as was physically possible. And her vagina was quivering with excitement, agitating the entire length of its companion-piece. Now it was this member that was incipient.

Prior let go her breasts and moved his hands down to her hips. He held her bottom tight while he kneaded her inner thighs and but-tocks and accelerated all his tools. He wrestled her entire torso about, half-lifting it, impaling it on the fork behind while her mouth struggled to subdue the whiplashing rod ahead. His entire gut seemed to gather itself for the building effort: prostate, seminal vesicle, kidneys, blad-der and colon interacting to produce a potent liquid lava. His heart pumped raw serum down through the arteries to mix with the sperm cells swimming up from the steaming testicles. A boiling pool of ejacu-late formed, swelled, pressed behind the safety-cock—

HOLD! he cried to his system.

In that physical and chemical and emotional pause he planted his two thumbs against her pulsing clitoris and pressed in, squeezing the little organ unmercifully.

Oubliette stiffened as though electrocuted.

Then he burst. The valves flung open, the turbulent concoction coursed out. It rammed into his penis, split into three channels, blasted up each separate tube. Prior felt it spewing into the dual chambers of her ass, rising along the passage to her mouth. Urge after urge—and finally the vanguard spurted over her tongue. Only a few precious drops, after the split and the enormous length of piping—but it signified suc-cess.

That was when she came. Prior was largely finished, but his mem-bers retained tumescence, and he held them in place while she rocked herself into ecstasy. Both holes clamped about the two short mem-bers, milking them of the last boiling drops, savoring the hard-won serum.

As she subsided, he mashed her clitoris again, working it sav-agely between his thumbs.

"No!" she cried around his mouth-organ. But he would not re-lent. He kept his waning members jammed in place and continued exercising her button, wrestling with it and pulling it and twisting it.

She groaned, she cried—and she climaxed again. But still he did not stop.

Her third consecutive orgasm began to turn the tide on his own cycle. Slowly his members regained strength, wedged inside her heav-ing body.

"That's enough!" she screamed as the fifth climax hit her. "No more, no more!" But he was working up his own second heat now, restimulated by the violence of her involuntary motions. He was making her respond; he had a feeling of power, and this turned him on as much as her body and reactions.

She began to fight him, kicking out her legs and falling flat on the bed, but he clung like a leech, outside and in. "Bastard!" she gasped as the seventh climax tore through. "Sadist!" with the eighth. "Eeg demon!" with the ninth.

But it was not until the eleventh that he came again, and it was slow and painful and immensely satisfying though only two of his organs remained lodged.

Only then did he let her drop, his two penises sucking out limply. The long one was still stiff, since it was naturally rigid, but it was buried beneath one of her breasts and he was sure the small ejaculation had not reached its terminus.

He was exhausted. He felt like a spent balloon. But he had put this filly through her paces. A dozen jumps!

"You pass," she whispered as his dilute sperm drooled across the crevice of her rear. "You just graduated. With fucking honors."

Prior knew that already.

Chapter 19—Message

He was whole again, in a manner of speaking, and in a major respect better than ever. His 3.97 had been replaced by a galaxy of serviceable instruments that could plumb the depths of any woman. Never again would anyone look disparagingly at his ready member and inquire politely when he was planning to have his erection. If it was sheer size they wanted, he had it; if special effects, he had them. All ready the moment he plugged in his choice.

Yet he was unsatisfied. He kept thinking of his original miniature. It had never been much, but at least it had been him. He had had it all his life; he had screwed his small share of women and his larger share of token-slots, and he had beaten it when both distaff and tokens were in short supply. Maybe the little fellow didn't have an impressive track record—but such experience as he had had, it had brought him. He had grown accustomed to it.

And it had protected him from venereal disease. What more loyal service could he ask than that?

The new array was impressive; he couldn't fault it on any reasonable grounds. Size, shape, sensation—Oubliette had more than done her job. But dammit, a fuck wasn't real unless the penis was real—and all of these were artificial. So he was unreasonably dissatisfied.

He still wanted his own flesh back, cheese and all.

"Have a good time," Oubliette told him, kissing him chastely. "I've done all I can for you." And she had, both as surgeon and as woman. He felt like a heel for not properly appreciating it, and he couldn't tell her why. It was time for him to go, and he knew he should do so with appropriate grace.

"Yeah," he mumbled.

"You seem pensive," she remarked.

"Merely the thought of leaving you," he said with fake and ineffective gallantry. But that was at least half-truth; he did like her in or out of bed, and was certain he would miss her.

"If there is any problem of adjustment," she murmured discreetly, "and often there is, emotionally—we call it the post-operative let-down—remember that a cunette is defined as a trench within a trench, for drainage. There are other things in life."

"A cunette?" he asked, perplexed. "Sounds like a small—" Then he visualized a trench within a larger trench, or two sets of labia, and smiled. "Sure there's more," he agreed. "But it's not the drainage trench I'm concerned about, it's the drainage pipe."

"Sometimes a walk down the Eeg-trail helps," she said. She gestured toward the back of the grounds. "The statues are knowledgeable about both trenches and pipes, and provide excellent advice."

"Uh, sure, thanks," he said, not seeing much point in traipsing by the erotic stone figures again. Maybe *she* found solace in such contemplations (on her way to fuck with the Eggers: ah, jealousy!), but this could hardly bring back his natural penis. Only her sister Tantamount could do that—and she would never give up her handy-dandy little anti-VD smegma producer.

"They do have their price, though," Oubliette said as she left him. She had, of course, other appointments demanding her attention.

Prior went to his car and drove, knowing that he could not escape the problem by traveling. He brooded. So he could go back to his regular job with the parking department, if he hadn't been fired in the interim, and market the tamponer on the sly. And exercise a different penis every night. Great life!

Finally, ridiculously, he turned the car about and drove back. He parked behind Oubliette's residence and took a walk down the path, as she had recommended.

The beautiful stone nude was still there, though her cold arms now stretched out as if to embrace a man, and her carven lips were puckered as for a kiss, and her pelvis pressed forward. If ever a statue were ready for sexual love, this was the one.

"What the hell," he muttered. "You're worse off than I am; might as well give you something to think about." He opened his fly and took the six-incher from its box and attached it. He contemplated the statue's perfect form and imagined it as a living woman until his member came erect. Then he stepped into the female embrace.

The stone was cold, but not uncomfortably so, and anyway he was clothed except for particular areas. He bent his knees and got his member wedged against the rigid cleft, nudging the deep vagina. He could not force an entry, of course, for the slit was inflexible and this penis was too large, but he could touch. He put his arms about her body and pressed his front against those statuesque breasts. He bent his head and touched his lips to hers.

The stone became warm. He felt it on his mouth and then in his hands and finally against his pressing penis. The hard lips seemed to become soft, as though responding to his kiss. He did not question this; indeed it was not wholly unexpected, considering the peculiarities of these statues. They had to be alive, in some obscure manner.

He parted his lips on hers and poked his tongue between. It met her tongue—warm, moist, animate. As he did this, her torso seemed to flex under his hands and her vulva softened similarly. His member nudged into her warming cleft, melting the inner stone as it progressed.

Prior kissed her again, deeply—and the way opened and the rest of his organ slid into her snug vagina. He thrust, withdrew, thrust, holding the kiss, clasping the bended torso, leaning against that bosom—and suddenly fired a liquid salvo into her chamber.

As he disengaged from her, feeling the hardness of the stone already returning, her lips formed something like the configuration of a spoken word. Her magnificent breasts heaved gently. "Go," she said succinctly.

That was all.

Prior unplugged his member and knocked the dottle out and zipped up his fly. "Thank you," he said to the statue. "You are an excellent lay, even if vertical. I go."

She was cold and rigid again, but there was a half smile on her lips, half a wink to her eye.

He walked on until he came to the statue of the man. The stone erection remained, but now the figure was bent as though inserting his member into a ready orifice.

"So that's the way it is," Prior said. "Well, what must be, must be."

He squatted before the statue, licked his lips, and applied his mouth to the forward projection. At first lick the stone was cold, as before, but it soon began to soften. Prior took the large glans in his mouth and sucked, and the thing became tender. He worked his lips down around the shaft, and the warmth descended with him. The penis began to throb.

Something cold touched his head. Startled, Prior paused. It was the statue's hand, unmoving yet pushing his forehead back. He sighed. "I was afraid of that."

He did not like pederasty, yet he did want his natural penis back, and Oubliette had warned him that the statues had their price. Maybe, however, he could fake it, this time. He stood, unsnapped his belt, dropped his trousers and shorts, bent over, and backed up to the living extremity.

The stone penis had solidified some in the few seconds it had been neglected, and the glans was cool and hard as it touched his buttock. Prior shifted, and the firm organ slid into his crack. Quickly it warmed again and became slick, as though coated with grease. Yes—this was what the stone man wanted.

Prior waited a moment, then leaned back against the member. But he kept his anus puckered tight, instead letting the half-stone member push down between his clamped-together legs, shoving Prior's scrotum out of the way. With luck, that would feel like the buggery it was intended to be. He worked his thigh muscles and jogged a bit in the rod, and in due course the statue came. It was a jet of icewater, squirting out in front of him. Better that than hot lava.

He pulled himself off as the stone cooled and hardened. Had he fooled the statue? He listened to the slowly pursing lips. "To," said the stone man.

Good enough! "Thank you," Prior said as he donned his trousers.

The sheep-statue was looking toward him expectantly, tail lifted. By this time Prior had pretty well come to terms with the system, though as little as a month ago it would have been another matter. He wasted no time with foolish qualms. He unpacked the slender five-incher (because it was easier to erect in a hurry) and applied it to the ovine pudendum.

"Ba-a-a-ack up," he told it.

As before, the aperture softened, and before long he was able to deposit a moderate seminal offering. The ewe's vagina was, by the feel of it, very similar inside to a human one, and the experience was not really objectionable. He could almost appreciate why so many country youths preferred their animal female friends to the less acquiescent and more fickle human ones. Bestiality was frowned upon, generally—but this restriction had no doubt been authored by people who lacked the nerve to approach an obliging sheep. It was said that one of the venereal diseases had come to man by way of a sheep: one of the crewmen who sailed with Columbus, bringing this New World disease back to delight the Europeans. Prior didn't believe it, but it did make a nice historical story.

"Mmm-mo-o-o-u-u-u-n-n-nnt!" the sheep bleated as it hardened back into stone.

"But I just mounted," Prior protested. Then: "Oh—that's your word of advice. Sorry. Thanks." He petted her on the woolly back.

So it continued. The dog gave him a fine slurpy blow job and barked "Ice! Ice!" The stallion rammed about nine inches into what it thought was his anus—Prior was getting good at fooling statues—and pumped out its lather, neighing "Cream! Cre-e-e-a-am!" "Don't I know it!" Prior replied, looking at the stuff on the ground. The eagle and the griffin were more difficult, and he had to pause to recharge before making a trio out of the statue man-and-sheep duo. Some of the exercises were rough, but in each case he did what was necessary or faked it, and hoped his increasingly sore body would recover in a reasonable time.

He understood, now, why Oubliette was so tired after making this journey to visit the Eggers. He, at least, could change into a fresh penis every time; she had to stick with her natural equipment. He wondered what information she needed, to prompt such an excursion every month or so. Or was it merely her generous nature, bringing physical joy, however transitory, to her menagerie and to the horny Eggers?

At last he had the complete message:

GO TO MOUNT ICECREAM. CLIMB THE CHERRY TREE.

And directions how to get there, and what else to do.

Prior contemplated his notes, rubbed chapstick on his chapped anatomy, threw away a bitten penis-unit, washed his mouth out three times with cold water, and combed the animal refuse out of his hair. Then he walked the short remaining distance to the cabin of the Eggers.

He knew that a different man would be there, for the Earthside layover was only a few days for each, but that didn't matter. The Eggers knew how to travel between the stars, and Prior needed their help.

For the Cherry Tree was on Mt. Icecream, and Mt. Icecream was on a planet circling a star not even visible from Earth. He had to take the Eggers' pass.

But at the end of this devious route lay the solution to his problem. The hazards were fantastic and the concomitant chores tedious, but he could win his natural penis back.

If he was man enough with the prosthetics.

Part 3:

The Cherry Tree

Chapter 20—Mount Icecream

Six of them began that grim trek toward disaster and disillusion. The Kid had started it, his adolescent chatter like a match that touched the right tinder after sputtering futilely for half a lifetime. Miles Long was his name, and Prior could see the scars on his psyche. The Kid must have learned to fight at the age of three and how to sneer at four. Prior, with a scar of his own where it didn't always show, would have felt more sympathy if the brat wasn't so good at both.

Miles (the Kid) Long had won twelfth prize in an Earthside Snapplepop contest by making daily collections from every other kid in the ward for boxtops. He had amassed about twelve hundred entries, and given in return a hundred and fourteen split lips, seventeen damaged teeth, forty-eight black eyes and two hundred and ninety-one substantive threats. When he won, he had opted for the tour: one week at Mt. Icecream. Naturally he had been bored crazy after the first day. So he thought he'd gain the fame he craved by climbing to the top, and the old fool Yale Payton had agreed with him, and the next thing there were five suckers clamoring for equipment. With Prior Gross the guide.

Prior had lacked the wherewithal to finance a jaunt through the Pass, so had had to make the best deal he could. Mt. Icecream Resort was perennially short on mundane personnel, so he'd signed on for a six-month hitch as caretaker-guide in return for a moderate stipend plus transportation to and from. He'd started duty three weeks ago—and like the Kid, he'd been bored stiff (without erection) after about twenty-four hours.

This was no piece of cake. It was a dish of ice cream.

Snow swirled bleakly ahead of them, the particles swooping up to cling messily to their nylafur outfits. It had a yellowish cast and sickly-sweet smell; that meant it was vanilla, or had been before the wind chipped it into crystals. The sugar tended to coat all warm surfaces, becoming more and more grimy as time passed. Human beings carried with them the bacteria of decay and the calories of body-warmth, and that meant perpetual trouble here. Eventually, with this rampant tourism, the entire area would be infected, and Mt. Icecream would become Mt. Rancidsludge, but no one seemed to care. Certainly Prior didn't. What was a little more pollution in the galaxy, after all? He'd had his fill, and not just figuratively. He'd had to eat a quart of ice cream every day, per the Resort policy of demonstrating that the surroundings were, indeed, good enough to eat. Yech!

He turned his head to check the party. Behind him was Stedman Awk, a fat, wealthy slob of a man who'd made his fortune in hamburgers (despite thirteen injunctions over the years against cutting the meat with chickenneck, fishheads, horsemeat and plain old—very old—stale bread) and now he wanted to see how the other half functioned. The dessert-racket half, specifically. And he had caught the adventure fever from the Kid. He would learn about a lot more than rancid ice cream before he got home.

Third was the lone female, Chloe Samuels, who claimed to be a specialist in something or other. It could have been interesting, having a woman along in a necessarily tight formation like this, but it wasn't. For one thing, she was dumpy; for another, even a beauty would have been unapproachable in this cold and grime.

Next was the old man, Yale Payton, followed by the Kid.

At the end was Ambert Black: a huge Negro with too much muscle and an unpleasant militancy. There might have been trouble between him and the Kid, but the Kid was just smart enough to know he was outclassed. Black was no amateur trouble-maker; he was a pro. He had figured to make the climb on his own, but Resort regulations specified a party of at least three, one of these being a guide, for any overnight excursion from the base. Black would have tried it anyway, but knew that the robot snowsleds would have cut him off. He hated meddling robots even worse than meddling people.

A motley crew, Prior thought, without a doubt. An old man, a fat man, an adolescent, a bitter Black and a dumpy doll. All come to see the fabulous mountain of ice cream—and finding it as motley as themselves.

Prior peered ahead again, but the yellow haze cut visibility and hid the peak. Just as well; its beauty was ironic.

They reached the Stage One campsite in midafternoon. The days were about twenty hours long here and the gravity about nine-tenths of a gee, both of which fouled up visitors in subtle but determined fashion. Disorientation, irritation, even outright illness—Mt. Icecream was good for an hour's visit or a six-month tour (but not *very* good for either), but a week was too long for patience and too short for metabolism. As these characters would find out soon.

Prior knew the party wouldn't make it to the top. No party ever did. Probably this one wouldn't get beyond the Stage Two campsite. The old man would give out first, then the fat one, then the woman. Prior had been briefed on such dynamics, and was already an old hand. The Kid would stick it out longer, trying to prove himself. He would think it was manhood and courage he was demonstrating, but actually it was perversity and idiocy. The Negro—now, he was tough. Black wouldn't quit—but after Stage Three the party would be down to two, Black and Prior, and that was below the minimum. The robots would converge, frustrating human ambition in the name of human safety. So it would come to nothing, as it always did.

Unlike these slobs, Prior had reason to scale the mountain. Somewhere up there was the Cherry Tree—his lone hope for sexual salvation. Somewhere beyond Stage Four, reaching for the summit. He had never been to the top—no one had, as far as he knew—and his present prospects were bleak. The outside treks were better than the station boredom, at least, but their approach to the summit was illusory. To really do it he would need a sturdy and reliable party, and no such was to be formed from routine tourist ilk. If only a bunch of interstellar marines were to take their liberty here, or central European mountain climbers ... but instead there were only old, fat, flighty, fighty or female vacationers, the products of pampered or deprived society.

So here he was, playing out the charade again, letting the paying customers dream of saccharin glory, and grow tired, and quit, having shown themselves up for the feebly ambitious slobs they were. He, as guide, had to pretend that there really was a chance for them to scale the candy pinnacle despite their drastic limitations.

Stage One was large, built to accommodate the many parties that did make it this far. To a considerable extent it was an extension of the main camp; it had electric power and a furnace and half a dozen private cubicles. Usually one or two couples would take the hike as a pretext to spend the night alone: "Hey! Know what we did? We made love halfway up Mt. Icecream! Match *that*, Jones!" The guide filled in for the rule of three, and for the price of a generous tip made himself inconspicuous when that became crowded. Prior had already escorted several of these liaisons, and knew that the anticipated adulterous pleasures too often became guilty quarrels, victim in part to the planetary forces of weight and cycle. Nothing like lack of sleep or a queasy stomach to heighten discord. Maybe sometime he would get to guide a pair of young women; that could be worthwhile, if they weren't lesbians.

But there was none of that this time. No coupling—not with Chloe as unattractive as she was, and no fairies among the men. There wasn't even much bickering, to his surprise. This ramshackle group actually seemed to be unified by a common purpose. He was sure it wouldn't last.

Tonight they talked. Chloe—Klo, she insisted on being called—was a better conversationalist than were most women, perhaps because she was physically unattractive. She didn't seem to be on the make for a man. Her hair, in the nightlight, was red—the too—sharp red of dye, but colorful all the same. She was fast on the uptake, with a snappy rejoinder for any remark tossed her way. The big Negro, Ambert Black, seemed to take half a shine to her, and that was funny too, because he was a true believer in racial purity. *Black* purity; none of that lily-white dilution of the stock. And the old man and the Kid continued to hit it off.

Prior thought about Oubliette and her peristaltic vagina, and daydreamed of shoving the twelve-incher into that orifice, foot by foot. God! What was he doing here on this sickenly edible mountain, when the real eating was back on Earth and between her legs.

"Sure, I know how you feel," the oldster was saying to the Kid. "My moniker isn't much better. Yale—how many times do you suppose I've been told to 'lock it up' or 'take it to college'? Actually my name means 'payer'; it's just coincidence there are other things called that. But every schnook thinks it's so terribly original to—you know."

Yes, the Kid had found a friend in the least likely place, and Prior knew Miles Long's impetus to climb the mountain had abated. The Kid thought he wanted to prove himself to all mankind, but one person sufficed. How many aggressive causes were just that way, sublimations for ordinary satisfactions denied? Prior revised his estimate: the old man would drop out first, but the Kid would join him, the fat man making up the trio.

Now he thought back to Tantamount, twin sister of Oubliette. Too bad she was scientist first, woman second; she had the body to give a man a real lift. Had Prior known then what he knew now, he would have thrown her down on that lab table and cooled his erection in her body before she even had the chance to get the loaded tampon out, and bugged out of there forever.

But when he slept, it was of the succubus he dreamed, there at the beach. She was neither man nor woman, that demon; but when she assumed the female form she was one hell of a fuck.

He woke as his penis-socket spewed into the blanket. He'd had a wet dream, but he wasn't even wearing an organ. Depth of ignominy.

Chapter 21—Black and White

Next day was a harder trek. The sun was out and the surface of the ice cream melted, mucking up their boots and becoming disgustingly slippery. Fat Stedman took a heavy spill about midday, soaking his bottom in liquid strawberry, and that was it. Yale and Miles decided to sacrifice their ambition in order to see him back, generously. Of course there didn't have to be a trio going back, because the alert robots would zero in on any lesser group and take it back anyway. But it was Prior's job not to mention such details. After all, these were paying tourists, and their pride would be salved by making it back on their own.

Now they were three, and the next dropout would terminate the project. That would be Klo. Prior could see she was already tired. She had been tempted to go back, obviously, but probably had realized that she had waited too long, and now the onus for termination of the excursion would be on her. For what that was worth.

Ahead of them Mt. Icecream towered in all its sugary splendor: the pinnacle a mile above the base camp in elevation, many miles on the slant, and many leagues by foot. Red, green, blue and brown overlaid its yellow underbase, with black and gray streaks coursing down like lava from a volcano. The red would be strawberry or cherry, the green pistachio or lime, the blue blueberry, the brown chocolate, and the streaks syrups of assorted flavors. All genuine and of excellent quality, up here where it was uncontaminated by the germs of man. The substance of Mt. Icecream would have carried a snobbish price tag in any store on Earth. Very little was exported, however, because the expense of shipping was greater than that of manufacturing an equivalent grade locally. A few super-snobs made a point of serving it on special occasions, but that came under the heading of conspicuous consumption. Every so often, these past three weeks, Prior had gone out with the shovel and scooped up some particular flavor on order for Earth shipment. But this was a standing joke among personnel and tourists alike: after all, it was only ice cream.

Klo saw him looking, and came up beside him. "It *is* beautiful, in its grisly way," she remarked. 'What do you think made it?"

"God made it," he said. It was the standard ploy, straight from the guide manual. The fact was, no one knew who had made it or who maintained it. It did seem to be beyond coincidence for the flavors and constituents to match Earthly standards so precisely, yet there was no possible connection. It was just here, and had to be accepted on that basis.

Ambert Black came up too, as ornery as ever. "Big benign whiteass God with a long whiteass beard," he said sarcastically. "Got nothing better to do than make a mountain of upperclass ice cream. Probably shits it in His off-moments. Why worry about unimportant little things like war and poverty and disease?"

"Maybe God's tired," Klo said, unoffended. "Time for a change in administrations."

Black was silent a moment, uncertain whether she was agreeing with him or ridiculing him. Prior wasn't sure either, but did appreciate how neatly she had thrown the big Negro off balance.

"Maybe God ain't just tired," Black said at last. "Maybe He's dead. And his last Will & Testament was to be buried under an everlasting pile of ice cream. Maybe it's every man for himself, now."

"Makes sense," she agreed amicably.

Black shut up, still not sure which side she was on. Maybe he felt a dawning kinship with her—and maybe he was afraid of that, Prior thought. In many ways, the plain white women of the species had it as bad as the strong black men.

They continued climbing. As elevation increased, temperature decreased, despite what people said about warm air rising. The greater labors required in the steepening ascent kept them all sweating inside their wrappings, however. Klo was red-faced, and neither from the light of the waning sun nor from any embarrassment; her breath fogged out in a noisy bellows-rush. But she wouldn't give up.

They made Stage Two. Even Black admitted his fatigue. He stripped without ceremony and plunged into the warm shower. He had enormous muscles, stout haunches, numerous scars, and a massive hanging ebony penis.

Klo just lay flat for ten minutes, getting her wind, and in that position she didn't look bad at all. Her stomach slimmed down, her breasts stood out on her heaving chest, and her facial features softened. Then she sat up and began peeling off the layers.

Prior was breaking out the staples, for the guide on such parties was also necessarily the cook and chief handyman. He watched, frankly curious to see what a dumpy woman looked like in the nude.

"Not as bad as I thought," he said as she got there. "You are overweight, but there's muscle in your legs where it counts, and your breasts are even handsome."

He thought she'd blush or get mad—he hardly cared which—but she just shrugged and got up to find the shower. "Get out, you scorchskinned phony," she yelled in to Black. "You can't hog the only facility forever. My turn coming up."

"I'll get out when I'm ready, you whiteassed whore!" the man yelled back jovially.

Klo pushed through the curtain and stepped into the shower with him. "Get out when you're ready, then, black woodpecker." Prior paused again in his preparations. Either he'd have to fetch the first-aid kit in a hurry, or this acquaintance was ripening faster than anticipated.

"Say, I must be hard up when long pig starts looking good," Black muttered, sounding surprised rather than angry. "Long fat *white* pig, yet."

Prior relaxed. There would be no race riot for the nonce. Black had a weakness for stout women...

The water splashed. "Gimme that soap, Derby," she said, and the curtain bowed as she wrestled around him for it, not waiting for him to tell her to get it herself, whiteass.

"Get your boob off my tube!"

"If that's God, he ain't dead," she said.

"I *said* I was hard up! So it's hard and it's up. What's it to you?"

"Let me feel that." More splashing and curtain-bowing. "You're half-right. It's fairly hard and up."

"*Fairly* hard!" Black cried indignantly. "That's pure polished ebony ivory horn. You couldn't soften that black bastard with a white sledgehammer!"

"My white socket-wrench could screw it down, though."

Prior's interest in sex had diminished after the workout the statues had given him, but three weeks in the candy snows had cranked up his scrotum and put blood-pressure behind his pet-cock, as his last night's imaginings had demonstrated. This trek had hardly promised an outlet.

Ah, well. It showed that such things were unpredictable. He stripped efficiently, plugged in Monster, and parted the bustling shower curtain.

They did not notice. Klo was hard at work softening the ebony ivory with her socket, and Black was plumbing the depths of the long fat white pig in the vertical position, front face, while the steamy water plunged down over both.

Prior considered the openings, then retired temporarily from the

field. He was stuck with a twelve-inch erection and no place to cool it.
But he was merely daunted, not defeated. He had had experience with
grouped statues, after all.

He braced himself, then stepped naked out into the blizzard land-
scape of Mt. Icecream. The vanilla sleet cut into his skin and frosted
his fingers and toes, but melted instantly from the heated organ. He
scooped up a double handful and rubbed it over his mighty penis,
and gradually the monster diminished into a midget. He dived back
into the warmth of Stage Two.

With cold-stiffened fingers he unplugged the now-empty phallus
and set it aside. He unlimbered a unit he had never had occasion to
employ before: the bifurcate double-lengther. He locked it on and returned to the shower, forked member perking expectantly.

Chapter 22—Two-Horse Sleigh

The tableau remained. The white had not yet softened the black, but was making progress.

Prior limbered his two-headed snake and stepped into the shower with the pair already soaking there. That hot water felt extremely good, now. They didn't notice him, though it was now quite crowded. Their bodies were plastered together, chest to breast, merging at face and crotch, and the hot water coursed down along all available channels. Klo was stretched and Black humped to accommodate those connections, so that the one was not dumpy and the other not tall. It was working very nicely, actually. She stood on tip-toe, and her feet lifted from the floor with every slow thrust Black made, and her buttocks tensed and quivered alternately.

"A touching scene," Prior murmured, but neither heard him. "No sense rushing things, I agree."

He separated his dual projections and used his hands to curve them around the two-backed beast. First he concentrated on Klo's flexing posterior, guiding the right fork up into the dark wet cavity between buttocks and thighs. The preferred location was occupied already, of course, but the secondary one remained vacant. He didn't object to anal penetration, when it was not his own anus being penetrated.

He knocked against the tight sphincter. At first it resisted, but then, no doubt in response to the sensations of the moment, it relaxed, and he got the head of the snake in. Then that tense-quiver, tense-quiver rhythm as her toes left the floor helped him, and he worked up a respectable depth.

Now for the other half. He carried the left fork around to Black's back haunch and aimed for the secondary (but only) location there. Because he was already anchored on the right, he had to stretch to make the left. Fortunately the member had been designed for just such manipulations and was elastic. The tip reached target, and, after several charges, found its lodging.

Not a moment too soon! The long pig climaxed violently and the ebony ivory bastard triggered off in response. Both anuses clenched and puffed with the jettison rhythm, sending dual shock waves of urgency into Prior's crotch. He fancied he could feel the ejaculate galloping from the one body to the other, pressing against each rectal cavity and the member lodged therein. Prior was experiencing both halves of the orgasm, and was building for the most solid eruption himself since his prosthetic graduation.

Black, his organ spent, became aware of his other apertures. "What's this pig at my face!" he cried, jerking back his head. "What's this shit up my ass!" he yelled, jumping away.

Prior's left extension stretched like rubber but did not let go. Klo saw it too, now. "Snake!" she screamed, bolting for the exit. Her anus, too, was clenched like a trap on Prior's half member.

"Snake!" Black cried, echoing her. He seemed to be twice as shy of reptiles as she, oddly.

Black scrambled out of the shower, and Klo was pacing him. Both seemed berserk. Prior followed, perforce. The two halves of his penis remained hooked in the two sealed sphincters, and he could not detach it from his own side while it was under such tension.

Black burst out the door and into the snow, dragging his company with him. Klo skidded alongside him, then caught her footing and raced ahead. Like two thoroughbreds hauling a harness-cart, the black stallion and the white mare hauled Prior Gross along on rubbery bands stretching from crotch to crotch. The vanilla flew to the sides as their bare feet slipped and kicked. Then they hit a maple-syrup slick. Black windmilled, caught Klo by the left breast, and held his position. Prior's soles skidded on the goo. Now he was a water-ski amateur, his cord hitched to two live boats.

Klo's foot struck an encrustation of crystallized sugar—probably maple-sugar. She did a split and spun off to the side. Since she was the only one retaining secure footing, until this point, a splendid crash was in the making.

Prior's penis-head popped out of her bottom and snapped back stingingly. With half his forward pull deflected, Prior fell to the other side. Here there was an outcropping of pistachio that piled up as he plowed sidewise through it. This tension, combined with the shrinkage sponsored by the cold, was enough finally to yank out the other glans, and he rolled to a stop half-buried in green snow.

He was freezing. But before he uncovered himself he twisted off the bifurcate, shrunken member and threw it away. Not only had his orgasm been stifled, he had been hauled roughly and painfully from a hot shower to sub-freezing cold, and he had no one to blame but his penis!

Black trotted back, shivering. He saw the splay of pistachio. He pounced. "Got it!" he exclaimed, lifting the discarded member. "Fucking two-headed snake!" He inspected it more closely. He did a doubletake. He faced Prior, who was just standing up and brushing off the green. "Where'd you get this, Gross?"

So Black wasn't entirely naive about prosthetics. "Doctor named Oubliette Emdee, back on Earth." Prior shivered and started back for the camp. "Want her address?"

Black considered, hefting the member. "Yeah. Yeah, I do. If she makes these in basic black."

"She doesn't make them, she fits them. But she has quite an assortment."

Black became almost friendly as the three of them crowded back into the warm room, shaking off ice. "It ain't that I hate you less, you white cocksucker, but that I hate cops more."

"Nice to know," Prior said neutrally. It was possible to get along with Black if you didn't argue with him, as Klo had shown.

"Yeah. There's this squad of whiteass cops back home. Cops ain't *all* bad—I heard of one once that wasn't, anyway—but these ones— five, six of 'em—need a proper screwing. Know what I mean?"

"Six at once?" This man had big ambitions!

"Got to be, or they'll scatter. Every night they bust up somebody's crap game, grab the stakes, and play it out themselves. All them fat asses, bending over ..."

Prior laughed. "I'll write out her address for you!"

Chapter 23—First Branch

The third day's hike was stiff, but still Klo didn't break. Now they mounted massive projections of rocklike sugar crystals that crumbled treacherously when subjected to the slightest stress or warmth. The candy grime got into their suits and wouldn't quite melt and wouldn't quite dry. At the margins of neck, wrist and ankle it became the consistency of half-chewed taffy (which it was) and pulled and chafed. In the crotches of thigh and armpit it became the consistency of lukewarm milk-chocolate, the kind that melts in your hand not in your mouth (which it was), and sucked and gooed with every motion. In the hair of the head it became caked butterscotch pudding; in the hair of the pubes, caked vanilla icing.

"Up farther where it's colder we'll be able to use pitons," Prior said, for all the dubious comfort that was worth. Anything would be better than this gooey intermediate zone.

Stage Three was nestled in a chocolate crevasse. The chocolate looked like bare dirt, just as the distant pistachio looked like living foliage and the vanilla snow like vanilla snow. But the consistency of this chocolate was more like wood. The cabin roof was piled with purple-blueberry or black raspberry flavor, Prior judged.

"After this, the climb gets rough," Prior said as they scraped rancid rind off their torsos. "This is higher than most parties get, so it's no shame to turn back."

"I hear no white man's made it all the way up," Black said, with the accent on "white."

"I hear no man's made it up," Klo said, her accent on "man."

"Not to Stage Five, no," Prior admitted. "No human beings of any color or sex. The robots built that stage, and a couple of *them* were lost in glaciers or something."

"I ain't even going to fuck, tonight," Black said grimly.

"Who asked you to?" Klo demanded. "You attract snakes."

"Save my great black godless strength to put beautiful black Black on the friggin' white pinnacle," he finished, glowering at Prior. "First man to make it."

Prior laughed. "If we make it, you can step on the top first. You're the paying customer. I have other plans."

"Yeah?" Black looked at him suspiciously. "What?"

"I'm going to climb the Cherry Tree." It was safe to talk about it now; they wouldn't comprehend the reference anyway, or care one way or the other.

"The Cherry Tree! You mean *that's* up there? On top of ol' Icecream? I changed my black mind!"

"You know about it?" Prior asked, surprised.

"I'm a man, ain't I? I got a cock, don't I? But that sure ain't my kind of cunt. I ain't goin' near it!"

Prior was intrigued. "You'll risk your precious black life to climb a stupid mountain of ice cream, but you're afraid of a little tree?"

"*That* tree, yes! I don't mind dying so much, but I'm choosy about how my ass gets reamed." He rubbed his backside, perhaps remembering what Prior had done the day before, but decided not to make an issue of it.

It occurred to Prior that the talking statues hadn't told him everything. "I only want to climb it and get the spire at the top. You can stand back and watch. If I fall, I'm the only one who gets hurt. Then the robots will come and carry us all back down. What's so frightening about that?"

Black shook his head as he stepped into the shower. "You're a whiteassed pekkernosed candy-coated bugging stooge, but you don't deserve what you're headed for. I tell you this for your own cornholing good: layoff the Cherry Tree."

"Why? I *need* that spire."

"Like elephant turds in your beer you need it! And you can't get near it."

"I'm curious too," Klo said as Black emerged from the shower. The Negro hadn't taken long at all this time; apparently he was serious about not fornicating. "What's so dangerous about a tree—a cherry tree, yet?"

Black ignored her and looked at Prior inscrutably. "They's no fool like a white fool!" He pondered while he toweled off his robust torso and Klo got into the spray of hot water. "Hokay. I know a little magic—black magic, of course—enough to haul down a branch or two. Suppose I bring one here, so you can see it? Then you'll know."

"You can bring the Cherry Tree here?" Prior was excited.

"A *branch* of it, paleass. That's enough. You look at it—then you can quit, and we'll just sashay back down the mountain, and not break any ill wind about it, okay?"

"Quit?" Prior demanded incredulously. "Because of a look at one fool branch? You're nuttier than I thought, and that was pretty damn—"

"I'm *smart*," Black said, taking no offense. He brought out a red crayon and began marking off a large pentagram. "You got a notion that'll wipe you out—and not only in this life."

"For someone who doesn't believe in God—" Klo said, poking her head and one breast out of the spray. Then she saw the pentagram. "Hey! That's how you summon a demon!"

"Don't bother me, pig. This is tricky."

Prior decided not to bother him either. Black was acting as if he knew what he was doing.

The Negro completed the diagram, then brought out a package of powder and a candle.

"Talk of the dark ages!" Klo said, coming out. Prior was ready for his own shower, but decided to keep his clothing on despite the discomfort until he had a better notion what this was all about.

"The *black* ages," Black corrected her automatically. "Now you two stand back. I've got an amulet to protect me, but your only safeguard is this diagram. Don't step in it, don't get too close—DON'T DRIP ON IT, BITCH!" he screamed as Klo did get too close. She stepped back hastily and wrapped the towel about her. Black glared at her a moment more, then resumed. "When I light this—"

"Sure," Prior said, amused. Black magic, indeed! He scratched a wrinkle in his scrotum where some chocolate had lodged itchily.

Black set the candle in the center of the pentagram. It promptly fell over. "So it's like that, eh," he muttered. He lit a wooden match and melted the candle's base so that the wax dripped, then set it down firmly in the puddle. This time it stayed. He used the same match to light the wick. When the candle flame was steady he popped the lighted match into his mouth to extinguish it, stood back beyond the rim of the pentagram, poured some of the powder into his palm, and made a last check to see that Klo and Prior were well clear.

Black chanted:

FEE FOO FII FANCH, I SMELL THE SAP OF A CHERRY BRANCH!

BE YE GREEN OR BE YE BRASS, I'LL GRIND YOUR WOOD TO WIPE MY ASS!

As he chanted, he threw a pinch of powder into the candle flame, taking care not to enter the pentagram himself, and there was a bright flash.

As Prior's sight cleared, he saw within the pentagram a mass of foliage. It was a limb from a tree-and a single bright red cherry showed.

"There it is!" Black grunted, sweating.

"Sure enough," Prior agreed, not knowing what to make of it. It was the spire he required, not the actual branches of the cherry tree, and their removal from the tree wouldn't make it any easier to climb.

"Now will you leave Mt. Icecream?" Black asked.

"Because you tore one branch off a cherry tree by magic?" Prior chuckled, walking toward it. "What kind of a white fool do you take me for?"

"Stay back, idiot!"

Prior ignored him. He stepped into the pentagram and kicked at the lone cherry.

His foot never landed. The greenery metamorphosed into a tremendous demon-shape. A huge gray hand shot out to fasten around Prior's neck.

"So you'll grind my wood to wipe your smelly little pucker, eh?" the demon boomed, blowing sawdust in Prior's face.

Prior was just beginning to comprehend what Black had tried to warn him of. He should have realized that this was no ordinary cherry tree. How could it grow in perpetual snow, otherwise? Now he was in trouble.

"No, no!" he gasped, trying to free his neck from the crushing grip. "All I wanted was to—"

"To take my cherry!" the demon cried. "Well, let's see you try it, sucker! My cherry has never been breached by mortal man, but there's always a first fucking time, right?"

"To get the spire!" Prior finished, beginning to black out.

"To get the spire!" the demon mimicked. "As if you could mount to the divine dildo without first plucking the cherries off the five guardian branches of the Tree! Well, I am the least of those branches, and I have taken the cherries of better mortals than you, fool. I'll wipe your ass, all right—right out from your puny body!"

"Cherries?" Prior was confused, and the hand choking him did not facilitate his clarity of mind.

"Well," said the demon conversationally as he squeezed. "Technically they aren't cherries unless they're ripe and fresh and female, and most aren't, unfortunately." It gave Prior's neck another painful tweak. "But you know what I mean. Unfucked." Prior finally twisted his neck free, leaving some skin and possibly a vein or two behind, and sucked wind. "No I *don't* know what you mean. All I came for—"

The demon put a talon in Prior's collar and ripped the shirt lengthwise. "All you came for was to grind my wood. Ha ha. Well, grind, mortal, *grind!*" It ripped Prior's trousers open, the claw narrowly missing a testicle. "Shit, mortal—not only are you deficient in wit, charm, and personal hygiene, you're missing a copulatory organ! Wait till I tell my siblings about *this!*"

Prior still didn't quite understand what was going on, but was sure he didn't like it. He was naked now, and of course the demon had never been clothed. And the demon had a fat nine-inch phallus stiffened for business.

Prior tried to pull away and get out of the pentagram, but the demon tripped him and sent him sprawling. Prior tried to roll, and the demon kicked him back. It was, in fact, a game of cat and mouse; the demon couldn't help chuckling every time Prior's chance at escape turned out to be illusory.

Prior noticed, however, that the cheery cherry demon stayed well clear of the burning candle. Maybe the thing really was made of wood, and would go up in smoke—literally—if ignited.

Prior reached for the candle. But the demon, no fool, was too quick for him. It caught his foot, twisted it, and threw him down prone with the step-over toe hold. "Hey!" Prior screamed inanely.

"Sorry—business before pleasure," the demon grunted regretfully. "Much as I'd like to play with you longer—chew your balls, bite your dong, squeeze the shit out of both ends of you, and all that innocent fun—I have to inflate you first."

Prior opened his mouth to scream for help, but saw that Black and Klo were staying well clear of the pentagram. They wouldn't come in after him. This wasn't betrayal so much as common sense. It was his own fight, brought about by his own stupidity in blithely entering the forbidden diagram.

The demon positioned itself, its heavy limbs holding down Prior's own. It leaned forward and banged woody fists into Prior's thighs. "Get them open, flab hole—I can't see your cherry." And the trunklike penis rammed into a tender buttock. Prior felt as though he were being impaled on a dull stake.

In fact, he finally had the message. He was about to get raped.

"You see, only the unfucked can hope to attain the Spire," the demon said conversationally as it zeroed in for another shot. "That's the way it is. So we five branches eliminate threats by fucking everything that approaches. Beautifully simple, is it not?"

The demon shifted about in order to gain better penile leverage—and in so doing released the submission hold on Prior's leg. This happened just as Prior realized the truth about cherries. This coincidental (?) juxtaposition galvanized him; he jumped and scrambled so suddenly that the demon was caught offguard.

Prior somersaulted out of the pentagram where the demon could not follow. "Gee, it was a virgin hole, too," the creature lamented. "Unsoiled by anything other than shit, water, a few fingers—and an Eeg egg." It nursed its disappointed phallus. "An only slightly tarnished cherry."

"Good for you, white turdling!" Black exclaimed. "You won through on your own. Now I can banish the branch and—"

"Leave it there!" Prior gasped, suddenly determined. The notion of getting mutilated or killed had been bad enough, but the threat against his assiduously-defended rectum had made him really angry. He dived for his supply pack.

"What are you doing?" Klo cried apprehensively. "Don't you know when to quit? That thing might break out and screw us all!"

Literally, Prior now knew. But this didn't change his mind. He plunged a hand in and brought out the twelve-incher. He clapped Monster to his socket and waited while it burgeoned. "I came to climb the Cherry Tree, and this branch sure needs some climbing."

"Man!" Black said admiringly as the pigskin towered turgidly, vaguely resembling a football in its full formation.

Prior marched toward the pentagram, phallus clearing the way like a snowplow. "Now I'm armed, you manfucking woodpecker! Come and get it!"

The demon seemed daunted, for Prior's fighting member was longer by three inches and leather-tough. But the spell and diagram kept the supernatural creature there, and this was its fucking business.

Prior stepped into the combat zone again, leading with that massive genital bludgeon. The demon's nerve broke; it was out-gunned. It tried to run, but bounced off the invisible shield outlined by the pentagram and fell, its front scorched. Prior strode forward and caught it from behind, reaching a hand down and under to grasp the hanging testicles and yank the entire loin back. With his free hand he hauled one of the large gray arms around, tweaking those demonic balls when he encountered resistance. Soon he had the demon's hands and feet together, and tied them in one bundle with the remains of his torn trousers: wrists and ankles crossed under the clumsy knot.

Now the demon got over its momentary shock and struggled earnestly, but that delay had been fatal for it. Prior wrestled the folded posterior into an upright posture and applied the pulsing tip of Monster to the demon's anus. The sphincter resisted, so Prior stepped back and kicked it with his snowboot, leaving a smear of caked vanilla across the hole. The muscle loosened only enough to fire a gaseous stench at him, then sealed as tightly as before. The demon flesh was tough!

"So it's like that, is it?" Prior muttered as he choked on the fumes. He picked up the candle and applied the flame to the aperture. "Fart again, why don't you!"

The demon did, not realizing what was waiting. A blow-torch developed as the gas hit the fire, and Prior had to reel back before he got singed. But first he jammed the blazing candle-wick into the open rectum.

The demon howled. Its body distended, blimplike. Flame shot out of its ears. Then the candle blasted out of its ass and accelerated like a rocket toward the ceiling, leaving a trail of thick smoke.

Prior launched himself at the rectum again, and drilled in with Monster before the sphincter could recover. It was like a furnace inside the demon, but he gritted his teeth and rammed in every inch before he began bouncing.

"Fee foo fii fanch!" he chanted in time to the beats. "I smell the sap of a cherry branch!"

"Mercy, you fucking bastard!" the demon cried as the odor of burning cherry-wood rose from it.

Prior might have let up then, but something about the phrasing of this appeal annoyed him. "Be ye green or be ye brass, I'll grind your wood to wipe my ass!"

As he finished the chant, he came, putting out the fire with living fluid.

The demon emitted a terrible scream as the first jet of semen struck. Then it dissolved in greasy reddish vapor. Prior was left spurting into air.

"You did it!" Black cried. "You beat the branch! You roasted its cherry!"

"Yeah," Prior said, contemplating the spatter on the floor. He knew that his victory had been largely luck—that and a brief combat rage that now was gone. He had never reacted that savagely before. Of course no one had ever tried to sodomize him against his will before, either.

Black was right: the Cherry Tree was dangerous! He wouldn't care to try battling another demon like that. His quest for his natural penis wasn't worth such macabre risk of life and limb, not to mention virgin anus. They would have to go back down the mountain.

"I thought you didn't know the score," Black said as he erased the pentagram. "But that's the finest fuck I ever saw. By a white cock, I mean. You screwed that cherry right out of existence! Man, I sure wouldn't stand in your way now! Let's go on up and smear the whole spook-ridden Cherry Tree with baby-juice!"

"Amen," Klo said. "I thought you were a eunuch, but now I know you were just biding your time for a real challenge. I want to watch it all."

And what could Prior say?

Chapter 24—Second Branch

The ascent to Stage Four was the roughest yet. It was not a far piece, but it was steep and treacherous. Prior had found new clothing at Stage Three, but it did not fit him well, and chafed in sundry new places. They used the pitons and ropes to scale a crystalline cliff, then had to lay low in the colored snow for two hours while a black walnut-flavored storm whistled over. The ice cream dumped on their heads was bad enough, but the pelting fragments of nut were like shrapnel, threatening to gouge out the skin of face and hands wherever it was exposed. In addition, their leaking body warmth sank them down into an underlayer of mixed sludge that became jelly-like around them. Prior would gladly have abolished all ice cream from the universe for all time!

They resumed the climb when the storm abated—and got caught in an avalanche of chocolate chip. The chips were like darts, then like stilettos, and at the height of it like fine swords, for the weather here did not honor dessert-bowl conventions. Black got gashed on the arm by a fragment weighing several pounds, and his cherry-colored blood stained his sleeve, but he wouldn't quit.

"To get cut by chocolate!" he grunted in disgust. "It's enough to make a fellow believe in white!" Then he looked about nervously, worried that the candy lightning might strike him down for his blasphemy.

"Probably there was an admixture of vanilla in it," Prior suggested as Klo did some makeshift bandaging. "That's what made it nasty. It was hybrid."

"Say, yeah," Black agreed. "*Pure* black chocolate would never slice me. *You*, maybe, but never me. Always trouble when you mix races."

"Can't trust halfbreeds," Prior agreed. No, it wasn't at all difficult to get along with the big militant, once he knew how.

They made it. Prior was dead tired, but it occurred to him that he might be better off tackling the four remaining Cherry Tree branches individually instead of in concert. He was not one of those men who could spurt twice in five minutes (except perhaps in extraordinary cases, such as the time with Oubliette) and certainly not four times consecutively, despite the fine array of weapons available. But if he could space each demon a day or so apart, and make careful preparation....

"I dunno," Black said in answer to Prior's query. "My magic ain't all that strong. I'm pretty much a layman, there. I might get the second branch here, but it could reach out of the pentagram some. And I *know* I couldn't handle the magic of the third branch, even with my amulet. You're strictly on your own there."

He considered a moment. "But with a dingus like that twelve incher, you can do it. Man, I almost came myself when I saw that thing start pumping!"

Every time Prior thought it was time to give up, he got unwelcome support for his quest. 'Well, I'll give it a try," he said, more bravely than he felt.

Black set the stage and chanted his chant:

FII FOO FUM FEE, I SMELL A BRANCH OF THE CHERRY TREE!

BE IT DEAD OR BE IT GREEN, I'LL GIRDLE IT TO JACK MY PEEN!

And the branch was there, its leaves green, its cherry bright.

Prior decided to stick with a winner. He had Monster attached and erect. He took a breath and jumped into the arena, grabbing for foliage where he judged an arm would materialize, and thrusting the phallus toward the anticipated rectum. He wanted to do this rapidly, before the demon had a proper chance to fight. That might spell the difference.

He found himself with a handful of leaves, his penis nudging rough bark.

Um. "So you won't convert, eh? Well, I can still core your cherry!" he cried. He picked up the candle and brought it near, hoping that he hadn't been tricked into assaulting a genuine non-demonic tree-limb.

Then the metamorphosis occurred, but quietly.

A woman formed from the wood. She was a dusky nude knockout—bold of breast, massive of thigh, classic of feature. She wore a necklace of little shriveled sticks, oddly incongruous against her physical beauty. "You wouldn't club an innocent maiden, would you, handsome?" she purred.

Black exploded with derisive mirth at the sideline. "Innocent! My uncle's cunt!"

Prior was taken aback momentarily, until he realized exactly what she'd said. Then he doubled his effort. "This is precisely the kind of clubbing an innocent maiden needs!"

He supposed that she would fight him, but she merely spread her comely legs with resignation. She had a remarkably neat genital region, not a hair out of place. Prior's member throbbed with something more than a sense of duty. "I'm really not in the mood at the moment," she said.

Prior was not to be put off by such conventional excuses. "You don't have to be, sister." He got down on her, on guard against a sneak attack.

"Not tonight; I have a headache."

"This is a sure cure for headaches," Prior said, orienting on her cleft.

"Yeah," Black called from the sideline. "Trade a headache for a pain in the ass!"

"But your organ is too large for me," she demurred.

"I'll just bet!" Prior hastened to ram Monster home before the demoness could strike, either physically or verbally. He gripped his phallus in both hands and aimed for the lush target—but the member found no purchase. Somehow it slid past the aperture and smashed harmlessly against her firm cushiony and exciting but nevertheless irrelevant buttock.

He peered between those statuesque thighs, parting the labia with his fingers, and discovered that she had spoken truth. Her inner cleft—her cunette—was ludicrously narrow, and her virginal vagina was no larger than the diameter of a knitting needle. There simply was no sufficient avenue for his tremendous penis, knock as it might at the portal.

"Now that you have tried and failed," she murmured with that same gentle purr, "I shall claim your formidable member as my memento of the occasion, my trophy." She gestured to her necklace that was now almost under his nose.

Prior suddenly realized that these were not little twisted twigs, but severed, dehydrated penises. There were about fifty of them strung together, some circumcised, some not. All had been hacked off at the base, and a few even had shrunken testicles dangling like beads on their strings.

His erection evanesced. What a bitch!

She lifted one delicate hand, and the nails on her slender fingers snapped out like the claws of a cat, as sharp as razor blades. "What a fine specimen this will make!"

Prior put his hand involuntarily to his crotch. His penis could be replaced, but he suspected that once she cut it he would have lost the battle, by the demonic terms of this quest. Regardless, he could bleed to death if she cut it beyond the socket-valve, for the plugged-in member kept that open.

"That won't help you," she said in a dulcet tone. "You entered the pentagram; you made a romantic overture to me, despite my demurrals. You may not depart until our delightful business together has been consummated." She reached for his shrinking penis, light glinting from those double-edged talons.

Prior lurched to his feet, but stumbled immediately. Vines encircled his ankles, holding him prisoner. Her feet had reverted to vegetative status—clinging, thorny strands. He kicked and struggled, but succeeded only in lacerating his ankles, while she hoisted her fabulous bosom and lovely head and reached her sleek, dagger-tipped arm toward his wilting crotch. She was in no hurry; she knew she had him.

"Here, you whitepekkered shitslinger!" Black called.

Prior looked up at this friendly hailing and saw the Negro throwing something at him. He caught it automatically.

It was the Pipecleaner model attachment.

"Thanks, Brother!" Prior called gratefully. And to the fair demoness: "Cutie, hold your trophy-cutter. I have not yet begun to fuck."

Swiftly he twisted off Monster and threw it aside. It was not completely flaccid and some blood squirted, but that couldn't be helped. He twisted on Pipecleaner and willed it instantly erect. The wide-open sight of her manicured cleft assisted this endeavor nicely.

The sultry demoness viewed the change and blanched. "That's not fair!" she wailed. "You changed weapons in the middle of the tourney!"

"All's fair in love and war, sweetheart," he replied. "If this isn't love, it must be war. Now serve up your sweet little cherry, 'cause I'm aiming to make the pie."

She struggled, but she was built for sex-appeal rather than combat—as all the finest women were—and her own vine-feet held her delicious posterior captive. Prior caught her wrists to nullify the knife-nails and pressed down on her voluptuous form. Her shape was truly immortal! As his moderately hairy chest crushed flat her surging female breasts, his thin long penis probed her twisting, twitching cleft. Now his practice with Oubliette stood him in good stead; he knew how to zero in no-handed on a pinpoint target.

Unfortunately, that wasn't enough. The channel was still too tight for the ship. He had range and azimuth, but the Pipecleaner bent painfully rather than penetrating that constricted orifice. What a minuscule hole, considering the complete and generous sexuality of the remainder of the demoness.

But that was the point of it. She wasn't *supposed* to be readily breached.

"So you figure you're impregnable," Prior grated as his crotch twinged again. "Well, I'm still going to impregnate you—or vaporize you in the attempt!" And wondered if that made sense.

He sat up, holding her at penis-length, and slapped her pretty face a bit, trying to loosen up that crack. Her head rolled back and forth, but she was laughing at him. She was demonic, literally. There was only one place he could really hurt her, and that was between the legs—where he couldn't penetrate. He couldn't even get his little finger in; he had tried. It would take a sledgehammer to drive in a pin, he thought despairingly.

Her feet became feet again, and she kicked them about, making things more difficult. Her nails were still claws, or maybe modified thorns, so he couldn't let her hands be free for long. He was getting nowhere. In time he would wear himself out—and it was a fair guess that she never would tire.

Still, there were positions and positions. This frontal assault was not the best for loose entry. Maybe some other configuration...

But he couldn't let *go* of her. Her hands were too dangerous, her legs too lively. Her toenails were barbed, too. How could he shift her about to suit himself under such conditions?

Well...

First thing was to distract her. To make her mad, if that were possible. How short was the temper of a demon? He held her arms spread-eagled and bent down his face, centering on her marvelous bosom. He took her right nipple in his mouth, sucked on it until it swelled ... and chomped down hard.

She yelped and bucked and cursed him in Arabic. Good, he thought; she could feel pain and didn't like it.

He wrestled her flat again and mouthed the other breast, but this time he didn't bite, though her torso was tense and stressed beneath him. He let her struggle and swear ineffectively for a while, then gave the turgid nipple a lingering lick and spat it out.

And made a lightning plunge for the rightie again as she relaxed, and ground it savagely between his molars.

She nearly bucked him into the ceiling. She was mad, all right. Fortunately she lacked the necessary cool for such work. She didn't like being teased.

Prior got to his feet, still holding her wrists. He forced her hands together and grasped her crossed wrists with the fingers of one hand. Her breasts flattened against each other and quivered like warm pudding, but she was too busy screaming obscenities at him to do what she should have: concentrate on breaking the grip. Even the words weren't very effective, because they were not in any language he could understand.

So far so good. He had her mad, so that she was not pursuing her best strategies. Now it got tricky.

Prior clenched his free hand, forming a fist with the knuckles pointed down. He didn't like doing this, even to a demon, but—

He punched her hard in the belly. Her knees came up as her

breath whooshed out, and for a moment she was unable to cuss him properly. He couldn't really hurt her supernatural flesh, but while she was distracted by the blow he caught her left ankle and brought it up to her pinioned hands. Then he leaned against that leg from the underside while he positioned his groin and aimed Pipecleaner for the definitive thrust.

Then she caught on to his strategy. But it was too late. Her hands were caught, one long thigh well flexed, and her little cleft stretched wide and taut. He placed the tip of his member against the clenching slit and leaned into it, using her arms for leverage to draw himself in farther. The action was all his.

This position was like riding a bucking bronco upside-down, but it was indeed better for penetration. Her tight vagina was spread to its widest, and the full weight of his body was hammering at the weakened portal, and her frantic kicking with the other leg served only to vibrate the skin of the orifice and work the probing needle in farther. It was still a very tight squeeze, but persistence was making the entry.

It hurt as he drove on and in, for she was very like the pencil-sharpener he had dreamed of. But what was pain, when victory was surging in his loin? Past her straining childlike labia majoris, pressing in between the slick labia minoris, drilling down into that puckered well—

She screamed as he distended her miniature vulva and greased the inner channel with his own preliminary lubricant. She groaned in real agony as he reached operative depth and began jogging. The fit was so compelling that a single bounce was sufficient to bring on his climax. And when the semen sizzled through the constricted conduit and sprayed into her most jealously guarded vestibule, she puffed into vapor and dissipated with a despairing sigh. He didn't even have a chance to mouth her tempting breast again; his teeth closed on cold mist.

Only the necklace of dehydrated penises remained, lying inertly on the floor.

Now his member was half-limp and stinging from the excessive torsion and friction as it dribbled on the floor. But he had conquered the second branch of the nefarious Cherry Tree!

Chapter 25—Hot Fudge Spring

The haul to Stage Five was something else. Glassy sheets of sherbet led up to a bloody strawberry glacier with treacherous mint-filled crevices. Prior had never been this far before, and he was daunted by the savagery of the unfamiliar terrain. Twice Klo lost her footing and tumbled into yawning sugar-crystal pits, nearly yanking both men in after her as the rope lost its slack. Once Prior himself missed a piton and skidded toward a noxious rum-raisin cavity, saved only by a lucky grab at a protruding stratum of frozen fudge.

The worst of it was that the climb was not straightforward. The mountain curved around and about, and was bulged with impassable boulders of icemilk and carved into deadly slanting valleys and jagged channels and shifting cracks and riddled with slippery fossae and ridges and thinly iced sink-holes. The wind was intermittent and spiced with cinnamon; now quiescent, now firing missiles of peach or walnut or chocolate at the weary mountaineers.

Toward noon the maple-flavor snow grew tacky. At first Prior thought it was the marginal heat of the lime-ringed sun; then he realized it was worse. They were coming upon a hot-fudge spring.

There was no reasonable way around it. They had inadvertently entered the canyon formed by the melting snow below the bubbling aperture, and the walls on either side were too sheer to climb, too fragile to trust. It would take half a day to descend and remount another icy face—which might be no better. His map was no good; up here the contours and flavors of the mountain could change with every storm. He should have been warned when he saw that fudge stratum—obviously left over from an earlier flood condition. Now all they could do was plow—or slog—grimly ahead, and hope that this wouldn't turn out to be as bad as it almost certainly was.

Of course, if the slope became impassable, then he would have an excellent excuse to give up his quest. No dishonor in accepting the inevitable.

Prior's boots sank into the chocolate overlay—first half an inch, then two inches, then six. He glanced back at Klo and saw she had taken another spill; her complexion was now a rich Negroid brown. As, perhaps, was his own. Thus did Mt. Icecream seek to equalize them all.

The mud continued to heat and thin. They squished through a level swamp of it, with the canyon walls overhanging threateningly some fifty feet above. They turned a murky corner and found the spring itself.

The chocolate burbled in the center of a pool twenty feet in diameter. At the fringes assorted objects floated—massed fruit-slices, nuts, candy, and solidified chocolate. Overhead the flavored icewater sides arched up into an almost perfect dome. Impossible to scale.

It was warm—seventy or eighty degrees Fahrenheit, here at the dribbling overflow. It might be boiling in the center. They would have to swim around the edge—if there was any viable exit above the spring. There didn't seem to be: The ringwall appeared to have only one aperture—the exit they had entered.

"I swallowed too much chocolate getting in here," Klo said. "I have to use the ladies' room."

"You mean you gotta shit," Black said. "So shit, sister. It'll come out healthy brown. But wait'll I get up current from you."

"He's right," Prior said. "Nothing will show under all this chocolate, and the stream will carry anything on down the mountain."

She looked dubious, but also in dire need. She began squirming about as though loosening her clothing under the surface. Prior consulted with Black. "Do you have any magic to get us out of this?"

"I'm strictly a summoner," Black said. "Pentagram, chanting, etcetera. I'm no magician. I can't do anything much here."

"Summon a fireman's ladder, then," Klo murmured, wiping brown out of her eyes. Prior wondered whether she had finished her nether business or was still in progress.

"Can't. Has to be a supernatural creature. They're the only ones subject to supernatural summons. And I wouldn't dare let any of them out of the pentagram—even if I could make a decent diagram here on this liquid shit, which I can't. Got your turd put out yet, or do you need help?"

She ignored his last remark. "We could make a pentagram on the surface, you know. Look—this white stuff is marshmallow. String this out between the five points—"

Black fished out an object. "Say, there is a lot of shit floating around here." He squinted, then sniffed. "Shit? This looks just like—"

"I think there's a sidewise eddy," Klo said. "I didn't know it would float."

Black looked disgusted. He hurled the object far downstream and wiped his hand off on his sodden shirt. "Livin' breathin' fecal matter shit!" he exclaimed.

"Healthy brown," she agreed.

Prior was too weary to laugh. At least they knew Klo had finished. "But the current would break up the pentagram lines," he pointed out. "Then the demon would escape—and here we are, chocolate covered."

Black scratched his fuzzy head, smearing more chocolate or similar healthy brown on his scalp. "No—I could keep it tight for the duration with a small subsidiary spell. But it still wouldn't solve the problem. How could a demon in the penalty box do anything for us *outside*?"

"It could drink up the fudge," Klo said.

"Say, you ain't half stupid, for a whiteass sow," Black said admiringly. "Even if your shit does stink of chocolate. But that still won't get us out of here—we'd just be at the bottom of the lakebed."

"Reverse it, then. Have the demon fill up the place with fudge, and we'll float out the top."

"And get carried down the mountain on a waterfall of boiling chocolate?" Prior demanded. "Too dangerous, and the wrong direction. And if a demon could do that, he'd use it to harm us outside the pentagram, and I'll bet that's forbidden by demonic law. Otherwise every demon ever summoned would circumvent the safeguards and abolish—"

"It ain't that simple, whiteprick," Black said. "Depends on the type of pentagram. Some summoners do get reamed, but I'm more careful. But mainly, some demons are brighter than others. Get a dumb one and the simplest diagram will hold him, depending on his strength. Now a Mephistopheles is so clever it don't even need the pentagram to haul your ass into hell; it'll talk you there, and—"

"Maybe we need a demon animal, then," Prior suggested. "One *we* can talk into—"

"I've got it!" Black cried. "I'll summon a hellephant! Always wanted to conjure one of those."

Klo looked at him. "An elephant? What good would that do? Anyway, you said you couldn't summon a natural creature."

"You and him just form up the diagram while I work up the spell," Black said excitedly. "This'll exhaust my magic, but man, it'll be an experience!"

Klo shrugged, chocolate dripping from her shoulders. "Let's mark off five points around the pool here, and work in opposite directions." She scooped up an armful of floating marshmallow and began spreading a string of it across the gooey crust. Prior did the same, shaping the stuff into suitable lengths. He discovered to his surprise that Black's subsidiary holding spell was already in effect; the lines remained in place as they were laid down, despite the slow current.

Chapter 26—Hellephant

It took almost an hour to do the job, but they finally finished with a pentagram twenty feet in diameter, anchored at the corners by icebergs of thick whipped cream. It swayed with the brown eddies, but did not disintegrate and always drew back into place.

"Jism spread on shit," Black said, shaking his head with admiring wonder. 'What a pentagram! Should get the award for novelty, even if I don't have power to bring the beast."

He got out his magic powder and candle. He lit the wick, stuck the candle in a floating crust of fruitcake, and sent it drifting into the pentagram. He began to chant:

FII FEE FOO FELL, LET'S GET RELEVANT!

GET THEE TO HELL, FETCH BACK HELLEPHANT!

And he wafted a cloud of powder toward the flame.

As he completed the ritual, a monster materialized. It resembled an elephant as Mr. Hyde resembled Dr. Jekyll.

"Who in the name of Heaven are you?" the hellephant trumpeted, stomping angrily in the muddy fudge and almost dousing the floating candle. "I just cleaned my feet, and look!" It held up a dripping brown extremity.

"All yours," Black said to Prior.

"All *mine*? But what do I *do*?" He certainly wasn't going to enter into any fornication contest with this thing!

"Make a deal to get us out of here. That was the idea, wasn't it?"

"But—"

"Oh, for pity's sake!" Klo exclaimed. "You timid men will never get anything done." She addressed the hellephant. "We want to get out of here. Can you help us?"

The hellephant peered down its enormous snout at her. "That depends on where you want to go, madam."

"To the Cherry Tree. Safely."

"There is no safe conduct there for mortals. The guardian de-mons fornicate—if you'll excuse the uncouth expression—any intruder out of existence."

"We know. We've met a couple. But you can get us to it, whatever else happens?"

"I could bore you a tunnel to the fringe of the Cherry Orchard, as it is not far from here. The tunnel itself will be secure. Will that be satisfactory?"

"See?" Klo said to the men. "Nothing to it." And to the demon again: "That'll be fine. How soon?"

"The construction will require about fifteen minutes. Usual terms?"

"Don't answer that!" Black warned her.

She ignored him. "What are the usual terms?"

The hellephant made a gesture Prior didn't catch. Klo blushed—and so did the demon, strangely. "Oh," she said. "Well, I'm not sure—"

"COD, of course," the hellephant said anxiously.

"We don't need no usual terms for no fifteen minute job!" Black yelled. "Fuck your COD! Make another offer."

But Klo had already come to her decision. "Yes, then. Usual terms. COD."

The hellephant made a motion like a bow. "Very good. Observe."

They observed. The creature faced about, stretched forth its trunk, harrumphed a few times, and began squirting hot liquid fudge against a section of the icewall. It was like the jet from a rusty fire hydrant. Brown fluid splashed away, but soon the heat and force of it ate a hole in the ice, and the hole grew steadily wider and deeper.

"I could have used that technique on the second branch," Prior murmured appreciatively. "But when does he suck it up? I never saw him inhale."

"Keep watching," Black said smugly. "The hellephant ain't no ge-nius, but he's a good, honest craftsman."

The hole broke through the first rim, and the fudge disappeared down it, draining elsewhere inside that makeshift vagina. But the hellephant continued to blast it forth, still never taking a breath. Gradu-ally the level of the pool subsided, revealing more of the elephantine body. The creature was squatting on the bottom, its hind end lower-most. It wore a G-string with a tiny patch in front. There was a turbu-lence around the base.

Finally the chocolate level dropped below the demon's torso, stranding the floating candle on a bar of brown ice. There was a hor-rendous sucking sound, as of three hundred bathtubs draining si-multaneously: gunk, gunk, GUNK! Now Prior saw what was happening. The hellephant was sucking fudge into its rectum and spewing it from its trunk. No wonder the thing never took a breath. But the supply of hot liquid had been exhausted. There was only a bubbling puddle where the original hot spring operated, but it would take many days for it to fill the pool again.

The brown jet sputtered to a halt. The hellephant sucked wind, choked, then farted bellicosely from both ends, clearing its tubes. Caked chocolate shot out, the refuse from its filters, and plopped down like so many bushels of diarrhea. Clouds of chocolate-flavored mist enveloped demon and people. Prior gagged, knowing where it had come from, but he still had to inhale the stuff or suffocate directly.

"I believe the connection is complete," the hellephant said politely. "Do you wish to verify it before making payment?"

"We'll take your word," Klo said. She turned to the two men. "Well, I guess I won't be seeing you..."

"What do you mean?" Prior asked. "We have to stay together, or the robots will come and stop our mission."

"The robots'll never get past the hellephant," Black said. "The demon gets very fussy about interruptions, once it starts."

"Once *what* starts?"

"She agreed to the usual terms, despite my advice," Black said. "COD."

"Cash on Delivery," Prior agreed. "Sure. I'm not stupid. And I'll pay her back what it costs."

"You can't," Klo said.

"Not C.O.D., turd," Black explained. "COD. As in cod-piece. He's the cod, she's the piece. Only more so, in the case of the hellephant. Much more so."

"Precisely," agreed the demon, removing the eyepatch from its crotch. Underneath was a tiny penis, proportionately—no more than eight or nine inches.

"COD—Cunt on Delivery," Klo said. "Everyone knows that." She splashed into the pentagram, removing her chocolate caked clothing.

"The hellephant only fucks once a century," Black explained. "But he makes that one count. He prefers human females, because they're comfortable, they don't have frigid cycles, and they live a fair spell. Most animals only get hot every so often, and are pretty uptight when not in heat."

"Yeah, I saw two dogs stuck together once," Prior said. "If that's what you mean by uptight. So the hellephant's fornication kills them? With a trunk like that, I'm not surprised."

"Of course not. He doesn't use his *trunk* for that. The hellephant is always polite and gentle—that's why most female demons won't touch him."

"Makes sense," Prior admitted, remembering what bitches the female demons he had encountered were. But he still wasn't clear on the nature of the deal Klo had made.

Klo reached the creature and lifted her chocolate arms. The hellephant curled its trunk carefully around her body and brought her in close. She scissored open her legs, and the demon's little member pushed up and in, not stopping until it was completely embedded. There was no panting, no preliminary byplay; just that matter-of-fact coupling, lubricated by liquid chocolate.

"Well, let's move on before the pool fills up again and covers our tunnel," Black said.

"Right now? In a moment that intercourse will be over. He's already all the way into her."

Black laughed. "It'll be a *long* moment, whiteass. Why do you think I tried to warn her off? The hellephant fucks for life—and she could live to seventy or eighty."

Prior gasped. "You mean—they won't *stop*? Until she dies of old age?"

"That's what I was hinting at, pale-prick. She'll eat, sleep and shit right there—and that cock will never pull out." He watched a moment more, then shrugged, accepting it. "She made the deal. She didn't have to, so she must have wanted it that way. Actually, I hear it's a mighty comfortable living for those who like COD. Cock onto Death, some call it. A pretty fair burial, too—the hellephant only comes when there's nothing left worth waiting for, when the fuck is falling apart, maybe two months after death. Then he creams up a storm and buries the bones in it. That's what I call a real send off—to be buried in your lover's cream."

"Yes indeed," Prior agreed, shaking his head.

They left the lovers to their stasis as the fudge spring bubbled up around them, starting the tedious business of refilling the pool.

Chapter 27—Third Branch

The fudge had cooled and hardened, leaving an opaque tunnel into the bowels of the mountain. And bowel was what the brown-caked tube resembled. Despite the solid ice under the solid chocolate, the air was reasonably warm here, and by walking swiftly they were able to keep comfortable without clothing. Prior carried his sodden outfit in a wadded ball under his arm, hoping to rinse it eventually in some clear soda stream. Where there was one hot spring, there might be others.

No such luck. The passage debouched into a system of icy caverns. Red stalactites hung from the vaulted ceiling, and similar stalagmites rose to meet them, like sets of teeth slowly closing. Prior broke the tip off a small one and touched his tongue to it. "Cherry," he said, noting the concentric rings of ice like the growth-rings of trees. "We're in the Orchard, all right."

"Well, get your rod hot," Black said, shivering. "Once we meet up with those three other branches—"

Prior nodded nervously. Fate kept impelling him forward into this challenge, despite his willingness to slide backward. He had vanquished the first two guardian demons—but how would he handle three at once? The moment he reamed one, another would be reaming *him*. But he had to make the effort, now that Klo had given her all for the cause. All her vagina.

The cavern passages led generally down, and fortunately they did not become killingly cold. Perhaps there were hot springs here, after all, melting new passages and imbuing the entire system with some warmth. But Prior didn't like the direction.

"How can we find the Tree, if we don't get to the top?" he demanded, trying to sound more upset than he felt. He didn't want to be trapped in here, but if they really couldn't find those malevolent demons—

"Tree's got to be in the orchard, whitepiss. Keep moving."

Unfortunately Black was correct. They traversed a cherry tunnel, stepped into a dull red chamber, and came up against a demon.

It was large and male, but its penis was stubby. "Who the potash are you?" it snorted menacingly, evidently disturbed from some private contemplation, as its erect and throbbing member indicated.

Prior knew he had either to stand up or turn tail—and he was afraid to present his backside to this demon, knowing what he knew of the propensities of these creatures. So with the courage of last resort he said: "I'm Prior Gross—and I've come to climb the Cherry Tree."

The demon frowned down at him, pulling on its penis reflectively. The organ jogged in and out like a telescope. "Have you any last wish before I dilate your puckered little ass?" it asked in the tone of a firing officer beside an execution wall.

"Just let me arm myself." And Prior drew forth the prehensile unit.

The demon charged. Prior had forgotten that there was no pentagram to hold it back, and of course the infernal creature had no conception of fair play. The bundle of chocolate-stiffened clothing flew out of his grasp and he found himself hoisted in the air, his member unattached. The serpent dangled from his hand uselessly.

"I haven't fucked a mortal into oblivion in years!" the demon cried zestfully. "But I wish you'd had the common courtesy to be female. Cunt is so much more lubricious than colon."

"Same to you, cherry branch!" Prior gasped, struggling to reach the floor and get some purchase. If he could just gain time to fasten on his member and whip it up into fighting condition! "Think I like to dirty my member on supernatural shit?"

"You need have no fear of that with me," the demon said, chuckling. For a moment it wavered into the cherry-branch format, but its grip on Prior did not loosen.

"You're overconfident," Prior said, feeling underconfident. "I defeated the first two branches, you know."

"That so? They were weaklings." And this demon's strength did indeed seem greater. It threw Prior down flat, put a bark-hard knee in his back, and limbered up that horsehung penis. It had not been, after all, completely erect before.

Prior's own member was still in his hand. He brought it down and shoved it under his hips, scratching for the vital connection. But he was face down with weight on his torso, and he couldn't get it attached without more leeway.

The demon poked a woody finger between Prior's buttocks.

"Let's see your touch-hole, runt. If it isn't big enough, I may have to widen it, ha-ha!"

"Ha-ha!" Prior echoed heavily. He tried to defecate on the demon's hand, but the position was wrong and nothing came out. Instead the probing finger got inside and scraped cruelly at the tender mucous membrane.

"I believe it will fit," the demon murmured with satisfaction, "after I enlarge it a trifle. Scream, please—this is going to hurt." Prior clenched his sphincter as tightly as possible, as the demon brought its loin down and began expanding its member. The greasy tip of it slobbered along Prior's scrotum before centering accurately on his hole. The demon pushed.

The muscle held. "Fucking position's wrong," the demon said, annoyed, but not completely dismayed by this challenge. It put bark-rough hands against Prior's hips and lifted his rear.

At first Prior resisted, stiffening his body. Then he realized that this was an opportunity for him. He bent in the middle, bringing his knees up under him while his hand jammed the prehensile member onto its socket and twisted it into place.

"Excellent," the demon said, breathing on Prior's elevated rectum. "An extraordinary neo-virginal asshole! You must really have saved it for me! I like this attitude. It makes it so much easier when you cooperate. Now we'll just fasten you in place—" It muttered an obscure pornographic spell, and Prior found himself invisibly clamped where he was. He could not budge head, arms or legs.

This demon was tough, all right. The others hadn't used magic on him. But Prior still had control over his sphincter. Probably the spell had to exclude that, or it would have been frozen closed, and be impenetrable.

Meanwhile his attached member was swelling rapidly. So the entire genital region was free, as well as his eyes and mouth. The battle wasn't over yet.

"Easy does it," the demon said, making itself comfortable behind Prior, dog-fashion. "First a little choice lubrication—" The ugly face moved down, and the huge canine tongue slurped over Prior's crack, wetting it down thoroughly with gooey saliva. "You've been consuming too much chocolate!" the demon complained.

"So what's wrong with healthy brown chocolate?" Prior demanded, momentarily gratified. So maybe he *had* gotten a little fecal matter out, and the demon had licked it up. Served it right!

"Cherry is better, as I shall shortly demonstrate." The demon chuckled. "Get that? demon-strate." But it became serious again when Prior did not laugh at the pun. "So you're still fighting it? Then we'll just brace against the portal and slide in a bit when it relaxes, so." And that slimy skinned-wood penis shoved, not hard but very firm and steady.

Prior kept his sphincter clenched, but the muscle was tiring. He remembered how starfish opened clams by exerting steady pull on the shells, until the clams could no longer hang on. In time that insistent pressure would wear him down, and he knew he would have no chance once the outer defense had been breached.

But Prehensile was finally ready. What luck that he had selected this particular organ this time! Prior curled it down between his legs, out of sight of the demon, then under his own hanging testicles, across behind those of the demon, and up. It looped in a three-quarter circle back toward the demon's rectal region. He was about to attack from the rear.

Now came the ticklish part. He had to make a good entry on the first thrust, before the demon realized what was happening. If that failed he would not have another chance, because his leverage was weak and his own rectum was on the verge of yielding.

Get ready ... get set ... THRUST!

Prehensile lunged forward, a striking snake, aiming blindly but with pretty good judgment for the supernatural anus. The azimuth and elevation and orientation were almost perfect; Prior felt the glancing contact of thorny buttocks, the bald alcove between them, the base of the crevice. He was driving for a hole-in-one!

Except—

Where was the aperture?

Up and down the veneer-polished crack Prehensile undulated, seeking its entrance—and there was none. From balls to back-bone, the demon's bottom was sealed.

"Ha-ha!" the creature bellowed. "Thought you'd pull a fast one, eh? Well get this, dimwit: I saw your friggin' worm, I let you put it on, and I near busted out laughing. You can't get me with that! Know, oh mortal—*I have no asshole!* You can shove and slither all you want—you can tickle me but you'll never nudge *my* shit!"

It was all too true. Prior was sunk. The demon had only been playing with him, letting him think he had a chance.

"That little torment was for fucking my innocent little brother out of existence," the demon gloated. "Now I'm going to get even for what you did to my precious little sister, she of the small sweet ripe cherry."

It brought its hulking head around, at the same time cuffing Prior's frozen body sidewise. Its face was grotesque: tiny near-spaced eyes whose whites were blood-red (technically, cherry-red), purplish wiry hair, monstrous flaring nostrils, pointed ears, and a chin whose cleft surface sported two sprawling hairy warts.

But it was the mouth that horrified Prior. The lips were black and blotchy, peeling back to expose jagged animal teeth.

"You tried to ram my rectum, touch my twat," the demon said. "Well now you can fuck my face." It crunched those devastating dentures together loudly. "See—I'm giving you more chance than you ever gave my mistress!"

"I thought she was your little sister," Prior said, his eyes following the thing's clacking jaws. His poor member would have no chance at all in a beartrap like that. But he could not move even one hand to shove the mouth away or disconnect Prehensile.

"Same thing. It doesn't count when it's all in the family. Not that I ever could quite get into her tail, in man-form. In flea-form it was possible, but then it wasn't much fun."

If he whipped Prehensile aside, Prior thought, those jaws would follow, playing cat and mouse until there was no further room to retreat. No doubt that was what the demon wanted. But if he detumesced it, he would still be disarmed.

The Cherry Branch meant to bite off Prehensile, then sodomize Prior at leisure while he bled to death. And there was nothing he could do to prevent it.

"Use your bleached gray matter, whiteface!" Black called from a safe distance. "Is that the best you can do? I thought you were a real fucker!" And the big Negro blew his nose disdainfully.

Black wasn't even a fair-weather friend. He had expressed nothing but contempt for Prior all along. Now he was rubbing it in. Blowing his ebony nose, while Prior was getting demonically chewed and screwed.

Nose...

The demon's breath was hot upon Prior's scrotum. The huge teeth hovered near the quivering glans. The mouth came down, smiling evilly. Slowly, slowly, tantalizingly slowly...

Think ... real fucker ... nose...

Prior launched Prehensile forward, a rattlesnake. The tip bounced off the demon's stubby chin, scratched nauseatingly against the hairy warts, skated over the slimy upper teeth scraping away a channel of smegma-like plaque deposit, skidded on the cleft of the mottled upper lip....

And plunged at last into the gaping left nostril.

"Oomph!" the demon cried, jerking back.

But Prehensile followed, thrusting deeper, wedging a passage through the caked snot inside. Three inches, four, five! The force of it slammed the demon's head back against Prior's raised knees, stopping the retreat.

Six inches, and he was well settled in the sinus cavity, warm and soft and slick. "Go, go, go, gonads!" Prior grunted.

In and out his faithful penis thrust, heating the membranes by the friction of its travel while the demon howled and clawed futilely at it. Then the Cherry Branch got belatedly smart: took a deep breath, pinched shut its other nostril, closed its big mouth, and prepared to blow its nose violently. This was a blow-job that would finish Prior—

Suddenly the spasm came, sending its fluid coursing along the winding hose and into the demon's pressurized sinus.

"HA-CHOOO!" the demon sneezed in agony ... and exploded into vapor. At that moment the spell abated, and Prior's limbs were free.

He had won again ... by a nose. Thanks to Black's seeming insults, which were actually advice couched in a manner the demon would not understand and counter.

Chapter 28—Fourth Branch

They moved on down the cherry caverns. This time Prior kept himself prepared: he had Normal, the six-incher, connected and halfway turgid. That way he was halfway ready for anything. Halfassed, as Black put it. But he hoped he wouldn't meet the fourth Branch soon, because the struggle with the third had exhausted him, physically and chemically. He wasn't certain he could get a full erection, let alone ejaculate!

"Well!"

Prior and Black both jumped. A demoness lay before them, dusky, sultry and sexy. She was another branch of the Cherry Tree, all right, for her cherry was bright red and sparkled between her supple, leaf-green-shaded thighs.

"Sa-ay," Black said appreciatively. "Can anybody play? I wouldn't mind cornholing that brown beauty myself."

Prior wasn't sure of the legalities, but his limp member cast the deciding vote. He might get it up for this encounter, for the demoness was as luscious a piece as he had ever approached—but what if the next demon arrived on the scene too quickly? Sheer glandular fatigue would do him in when he faced the last branch. Black knew he was not eligible to approach the Spire itself—but that was not his purpose. He just wanted a good fuck, and he knew the risk entailed. "Okay by me," Prior said.

Black needed no further urging. "Now you stay out of it, the way I stayed out of yours," he cautioned. "I know she's a bitch, and she'll kill me if she can, but this here motherfuckin' horn will not be denied." And, indeed, his erection was impressive.

"Right," Prior said, realizing only now that it had not been indif-

ference or cowardice that prevented Black from coming to his assis-
tance before, but the man's own code of ethics. Three was a crowd,
when it came to serious combat or fornication. Except for advice from
the sidelines.

Black advanced penis-first on the waiting female, took hold of
one arm and breast, dropped onto her torso and issued a pneumatic
sigh. "Just let me dip my stick in your transmission, black baby," he
said.

She shimmered—and Black found himself embracing a crocodile. Great and green and alligator-hided, with a thrashing tail and
elongated snout and cruel hungry eyes.

Prior, watching, was as dismayed as Black. There, but for the
grace of circumstance and a flaccid member, went he! He had known
the demons could change shape, but this was ridiculous.

Black, whatever his political sentiments, was sexually normal.
Bestiality was hardly in his line, when he considered it degrading to
sample the lubricity of even nonblack human females. Prior saw the
ebony penis losing elevation as it brushed the cold belly-scales of the
reptile. A luscious woman-form was one thing, demon though she might
be; this was something else.

But there was no release from that embrace. The crocodile's im-
mense jaws whipped around, snapped at Black's face—

But Black had brought up his wrist with the amulet. A blue spark
jumped, singeing the reptile's teeth. "No kissin', cousin!" Black cried.
"You can't hurt me. I got protection!"

"Human bastard!" the crocodile muttered, licking the charred
surface of the tooth. "Think you're pretty mortal smart!" And it changed
into a monstrous crab. "Well I'll just pinch you to see if you're real!"

Two gigantic pincers reached for the man. One went for the throat,
and Black had to fend it off immediately with the amulet.

The other pincer moved simultaneously for his groin, and Black,
distracted by the threat to his neck, didn't catch it in time. It clamped
on the genitalia and wrenched—and suddenly Black was a bleeding
eunuch. He screamed once, horribly, then fainted.

Prior was appalled, sickened, and terrified, but also angry. The
foul-mouthed Negro was his friend in his black-humor fashion. Black
had twice summoned cherry branches for him to tackle individually,
and had once thrown him a penis when he had been caught short.
Last time Black had given him the life-saving hint about the Demon's
nose—the facial aperture *without* deadly teeth. And Black had gotten
them safely here by summoning the hellephant.

Yes, Black was a friend in deed and sometimes in word. Prior
knew he could not have made it this far without the man's timely as-
sistance. Black didn't deserve such mutilation and death, when all he
had wanted was a decent dusky rock.

The crab metamorphosed back into the crocodile, and the crocodile opened her jaws to take another bite of manflesh. The dripping penis and scrotum lay on the cold cavern floor, the blood melting into the cherry ice.

Prior charged.

If he had had time to think it through properly, he would have known he had no chance, and let the Negro's corpse buy him time to escape. He would have given up his insanely foolish quest for the Spire. He would have returned to Earth a sadder but more potent man.

But now rage drove out all fear and all reason. His six-incher was not even rigid, but he tensed his legs to pounce on the crocodile.

His foot slipped on the severed, peeled-banana penis. A testicle squirted out from under as Prior fought for balance. He couldn't stop; he had to fall, so he fell forward.

And landed astride a tigress. Literally.

"Another lover, so soon!" she purred, her predator-muscles orienting on him. "Well here's some real pussy for you, halfmast!"

She twisted off Black and faced Prior, the deadly sharp claws of all four feet driving for his gut. But he still had some of the advantage of surprise; she was not properly braced for his impact, and the floor was slippery with diluted blood on the ice. He crashed into her bodily and shoved her sidewise, away from Black.

Instinctively he wrapped his arms about her torso, pulling her tight to restrict those scraping claws. And then she was an enormous fat hen. "Squa-awk!" she squawked. "Let's have some cock!"

He tried to wring her small neck, but the clumsy bird became an unclumsy bird: a giant eagle, its bill stabbing down at his eyeballs.

There was hardly time to react, let alone think. Prior butted his head against hers, using his hard skull to blunt her sharp beak, and reached out wildly for Black's body. There was sharp pain in his skull as hair and skin were gouged, but he found the body. While he fought off the buffeting eagle's wings one-handed he wrestled with the Negro's body for that magic amulet. It was set in a bracelet, and if he could get it off—well, he could take the punishment of claw and beak for a little while, so long as he got hold of that protection.

Meanwhile his opponent had changed her shape again. A man-sized hairy spider threw loops of sticky web about him while purple mandibles came at his face. But he got hold of Black's arm, slid along the wrist, hooked a finger under the band. As the spider's venom-dripping jaws opened to clamp on his nose, he hauled desperately on amulet and hand, and brought it between him and the demoness. The spark jumped again.

"Now cut that out!" the spider said, jerking back while its face-fur smoked. Its six or ten eyes blinked in pain. "I'm just trying to offer you a little good hair-pie." But already she was a shark, with seemingly endless teeth.

"There's something fishy about you," Prior grated. He put the

amulet right into that underslung maw and drove it back. He had a
weapon now—but he knew it could not win the battle for him by itself.
It had not been enough for poor Black. He used it to fend her off while
he concentrated desperately on his definitive weapon: his penis. He
could vanquish her completely only by copulating with her—and it
had to be fast, or he was dead, amulet or no.

But it was hard to stiffen his torpid member in the face of these
repeated changes of form. Now the bitch was a bear, now a snake, now
a pig. Each form constituted a new attack by claw, fang or snout, and
none was sexually conducive. And he sorely missed the semen he had
so recently expended on the assless demon. An amulet was no substitute for ejaculate.

Nevertheless the heat of combat elevated his blood pressure, and
his member gradually came erect. The abrasion it received during the
struggle helped, though there was little sexual appeal in this. As his
penis hardened, the demoness lost strength, for here was the thrusting phallus she most feared. Her scratches became shallow, and her
blows futile. Finally she collapsed back into human form.

Prior wedged her luscious thighs apart and forced his full-sized
meat into her loosening hole. At least this vagina was ample. He had
been half afraid she wouldn't have one. She screamed and went limp.

He had won again.

Except—

Except that he hadn't come yet. And she hadn't puffed into smoke.
That was suspicious.

She was playing possum, though she had carefully avoided assuming the possum shape, evidently hoping he'd be satisfied with the
seeming victory. She must have known that he couldn't come quickly,
so her loose vulva was safe for the time being. If he fell for that ruse,
who could guess what deviltry she would come up with once she recovered the initiative?

Prior rammed into her the full six inches, finding no resistance.
It was such a contrast to the vice-like tightness of the other female;
this one was a cool ocean in her laxity. In fact, he had precious little to
strive against, and his penis was freezing.

That was her trap! She was zero weather inside, and his hot
blood was rapidly chilling. He had to finish the job promptly, or his
flesh would go numb.

He couldn't come. He had to have incentive, stimulation, and
friction, and there was no more of these here than might be had by
having intercourse with a day-old corpse. In fact she even felt corpselike
now—a body in the freezer.

Black groaned and stirred. "Did you trim her wick, whiteshit?"

So he was alive! "I have it in, but the juice is congealing. Do you
have any more advice?"

Black coughed unhealthily. "My old man—curse his black hide—

always said…" He trailed off.

"What did he say?" Prior demanded. His whole front was getting chilled; he might as well have been having intercourse with a bank of snow. "Don't faint now, you bastard nigger!"

"Flattery … nowhere…"

"Listen, Black, I'm not flattering you"! My cock is an icicle! Tell me what you know!"

"If you can't eat it, and you can't…" The voice became an indecipherable mumble.

"What? What?" Prior shouted desperately. Not only was his member going numb, it seemed to be frozen in place in her ice-solid body. To withdraw now might well be to rip it off himself.

"… can't fuck it…"

"I know I can't fuck it!" Prior cried. "That's my problem! *Tell me*, you deballed wonder!"

"PISS ON IT!" Black screamed furiously. And died.

There went his last hope. Black's eleventh-hour help had pulled him through before, but there was no chance of that now. "Piss on it!" Prior echoed with mixed sorrow and rage. Why had he driven Black into such anger as the man lay dying? His thoughtlessness had cost them both their penises and their lives.

Piss on it…

Inspiration! Would it work?

He resumed pumping, pretending that there was still fire in his phallus. "I'm getting near the climax, you demonic cherry whore," he told her. "You're a corpse, but you can't cool my organ. Not deep down to the source of semen. It's sort of fun, fucking frigidity; a novelty, sets me off. You can't shrink me before I spurt. Feel that hot burble starting?"

"No," she said uncertainly.

He jogged his dead member, hoping it was more rigid than it seemed, and not because of getting frozen. "What an orgasm! It's raging in my gut! I can't hold it back any longer, much as I enjoy playing with you! You're quite a lay, know that?"

"You're quite a bluffer, know that?"

"Ooooh!" he cried, twisting his face in simulated rapture. "Ah, crocodile-cunt, I've never had one like this! Aaaaah!" And he panted and tensed his whole cold body as though torn by the spasm.

She changed into a giant, slimy, wriggling worm. But his member was wedged in the thing's cloaca, and he continued his act. "I'm coming! I'm coming! Swing low, sweet chariot! Feel that hot liquid!"

And he compressed his belly and urinated forcefully into her quivering vagina as she changed back into a woman.

"A-a-a-a-ah!" she screamed in climactic agony. She began to dissolve into chilly vapor.

Suddenly her misty eyes opened. "You unmitigated fucker!" she snarled, metamorphosing into the tiger. Her hole clenched airily. "That's not ejaculate!"

Prior just waited, letting his bladder drain into her, warming his cold penis during its passage. It felt almost as good as a real climax.

"That's PISS!" the crocodile bellowed.

But it was too late. She could not pull her wafting flesh together again. Slowly, reluctantly, angrily, and with multiple changes of form, she faded into brown, urine-saturated mist. His last drops spattered on the pink ice.

This time he really *had* won—by cheating.

Chapter 29—Fifth Branch

He buried Black in the cherry-flavored terrain, and found some chocolate snow for a shroud. "You gave good advice, you ebony racist," he said by way of benediction. "I'll take care of the cop-fucking matter for you, if I ever get back to Earth. Keep cool."

Black kept cool. He was frozen stiff.

Four branches of the Cherry Tree had been severed—each one worse than the last. Surely the worst was yet to come. But now he had to go on. He would vanquish the final demon, or die in the fucking attempt.

He arrived at last at the bottom of the cavern system, in the very heart of Mt. Icecream. Here he found a fountain: liquid ice cream spurting up from a tiny nozzle, shooting high up through a gap in the pinnacle, and fanning far above into perpetual snow. As he watched, the color changed from yellow to green: vanilla to pistachio.

"PISStachio," he murmured. "How appropriate."

Mt. Icecream, it seemed, was a cold but active volcano—and this nozzle was the apparent source of it all. It must have taken centuries for the mountain itself to form.

But what lay below the nozzle? Surely all that ice cream came from somewhere. Was the core of the planet made of it, and was this the only hole in the crust for it to squirt out? That seemed ridiculous on numerous grounds. But at the moment he found no better explanation for what he witnessed here.

He stepped close to that ever-jetting phallus, feeling the convective wind at his back, and probed at the base. There might be a pipe leading in, a conduit for pressured ice cream—

Heavy footfalls sounded behind him. Prior whirled to face the last branch of the Cherry Tree.

It stood about seven feet tall. It looked a little like a griffin and a little like a goblin, but mostly like a walking phallus with priapism. It had snaggle-tusks that projected from the place its mouth should have been but wasn't, and a wickedly hooked beak without nostril-holes, and saber-claws, and a spiked tail and barbed wings. Its upthrusting animal ears were metallic, with serrated saw-blade edges but no apertures into the head. Its grotesque eyes were mere patches of light-sensitive skin. Its penis was just about two feet long from bell to balls, and proportionately massive. And it was absolutely rigid.

"An eeg!" Prior cried, recognizing the form. "An adult eeg!"

The creature made no answer. How could it, without a mouth? How could it really see him or hear him or smell him, with those sealed-over organs of perception? Now Prior saw that it had no apertures of any kind, especially not a rectum. Just that atomic cannon of a penis.

Prior still wore Normal, and the respite he had gained by urinating into the last branch allowed him to bring it to attention with reasonable dispatch despite the lingering chill. He knew he could ejaculate, once he found appropriate lodging. But this demon was invulnerable, for it was completely without orifices. In all the galaxy there was no finer single-purpose fucking machine.

The eeg charged on stubby goblin-legs, its phallus swaying heavily as though about to unbalance the entire body. The demon's eye-patches glowed cherry red, and so did the tip of its penis. What internal fires did this leakage presage?

Prior tried to run, but his feet skidded on the ice and he sprawled ignominiously. The eeg came to stand over him, huge chicken-feet on either side of his body, that volcanic member looming. The intrusion of that timber would surely split a human body wide open. But there was no ready escape. The cold of the cavern floor gripped his naked body; was that why he shivered so?

The demon lowered the boom. That hinged instrument was as thick and solid as Prior's thigh. It banged brutally against his buttock, a solid wooden club.

Prior realized that he was in luck—of a sort. A penis that size couldn't possibly penetrate his anus, mouth, or any other bodily aperture.

The eeg reached down with spindly arms and hauled Prior up with astonishing strength. It carried him to a region of massed stalagmites: giant spokes of cherry ice rising erotically out of the floor. It jammed him between two of them, headfirst, and shoved him down, so that his torso was pinned where the columns came together at the base.

Oh-oh! Now he was thoroughly anchored. That huge penis just might get into him, if driven with enough force while he was tied down.

After all, the Assyrians used to drive wooden stakes up the rectums of their captives and mount them along the highways. And the eeg was bracing against a fortuitously placed third stalagmite, orienting itself so that its entire strength could shove the cannon into the recalcitrant hole. The eeg must have done this many times before; trust it to know its infernal business.

The club drove at Prior's posterior, harder and harder. His buttocks were bruising, his poor little sphincter was hopelessly outclassed. Neither flesh nor cartilage could withstand the savagery of this assault. It was like giving birth to a baby, sidewise—except that he was no mother, this was no baby, and it wasn't going but coming. In more ways than one.

The icy stalagmites chilled his sides—but his body heat was melting them in return. Prior realized that he had a chance here to escape. He waited for another eeg-thrust, then sucked in his breath and shoved back against those translucent columns with both hands.

It worked! He squirted out of that stockade, a human watermelon seed goosed by an inhuman battering ram. He crashed into another stalagmite, bruising a shoulder—but he was loose. He had another chance to escape.

The eeg made a mouthless roar and lumbered after him. Prior dodged behind the icy column. One advantage he had now: he was more agile. Much more of his muscle was in his arms and legs, while the greatest mass of the eeg was in its terrific penis. The creature was inherently off-balance; it had to lean back just to stand up straight, and it couldn't accelerate rapidly around corners.

Poor as its eyes and ears seemed, the demon obviously had an excellent notion where Prior was. Did it use magic to follow him so accurately? In that case, why hadn't it bound him with an immobility spell, the way the other branch had?

Prior could guess the answer to that: it must take some intelligence to master the complexities of magic, and the eeg's brain was only big enough to master the simplicities of fornication. And pursuit.

Prior scrambled over a mound of solidly frozen cherries, then paused to watch from hiding. If he wanted to escape this diabolic creature, let alone overcome it, he'd better find out what powers it had beside fornication.

First he heard a sniff-sniff, snuff-snuff. Oh? Was its nose perforated after all? Prior knew what to do in that case.

Then the eeg came into view. Its penis was leaning toward the floor, cantilevered, the bulging glans almost touching the ice, and the elephantine slit at the end was sniffing out the trail.

So that was the secret! Versatile member, there.

But if it was smell that gave him away, he was doomed. He could avoid the eeg for a considerable time, but eventually he would have to rest or sleep. He was sure the eeg, being basically demonic, never had to do either. It would never even stop to defecate, with no anus. It would just keep going indefatigably. In time it would surely catch him, no matter where he went, now that he had challenged it by entering its lair.

Prior whipped around another slender stalagmite—no, this one was a stalactite, hanging from the ceiling—and stumbled as it snapped off in his hands.

He righted himself and looked at what he held. A spear! He took the caked shirt he still carried and wrapped it about the basal end, both to protect his hand from the cold and to prevent the icy needle from melting. With this he might make his own hole in the eeg, and ram home there for victory. "Now come and get it," he snarled. "If you can come after you get it..."

The demon, too stupid to be cautious, approached. The penis lifted, centering on him as though it were a sword in its own right. And perhaps it was, or at least a bludgeon. Prior fenced with it.

"Touché!" he yelled, lunging.

The rapier scored—but slid off the penis. He lunged again—and was deflected again.

"Wouldn't you know it!" he griped. "Invulnerable meat!" But he made ready for another attack. Maybe a swift stab in the balls—

The eeg-penis burbled. Fluid squirted from its slit, striking the stalactite-weapon. The ice melted instantly, and the spear broke in half.

"Oh, no!" Prior cried, dismayed. He needed a metal rapier, and there was nothing here but ice. He fled, wishing there was a river or something for him to lose his scent-trail in, or some cubbyhole the eeg couldn't reach.

Then he remembered the mound of cherries. He veered back to it and used the stub of his sword to pry loose a handful. He wheeled and pelted the demon with the red bullets.

Then he noted that some were not shaped quite like cherries. He inspected one of these more closely—and discovered that it was actually a frozen testicle.

Well, they were still solid, stinging little missiles. He knew the strikes annoyed the creature, though they could hardly hurt it. Maybe it was angry because its trophy-collection was being scattered.

The mighty penis aimed again, swinging grandly around as though mounted on gimbals. Prior tried to button the slit with a well-aimed cherry-ball, but his marksmanship wasn't that good. More fluid gooshed forth, arching beautifully and descending to strike Prior's arm. It was hot and gooey and repulsive. He jerked away but the gob clung to him. He slapped at it with his other hand—and it stuck there too, stretching out between arm and hand in a glistening string, that cooled as it thinned and hardened as it cooled. It smelled richly of butterscotch.

Good God! This wasn't ejaculate as he knew it—it was taffy!

Prior lurched on. The hardened goo just would not come off without taking the skin along too. Now his mobility was seriously hampered. What if the next ejaculation struck his legs? Or his face?

He couldn't escape the eeg and he couldn't fight it. What else remained?

What else but copulation?

He imagined being reamed by that horrendous member, and half a gallon of boiling taffy being firehosed into his colon, and knew he couldn't surrender. He'd kill himself first.

In the midst of this noble sentiment, he slipped on a rolling cherry and went down on his face. This time he hit hard, because his arms were entangled in solidified taffy jack. Light and darkness tinged with cherry-red exploded in his eyes, and he knew he was on the verge of unconsciousness. An unconsciousness he was unlikely to emerge from before being stuffed with butterscotch.

One thing fixed in his mind: what the hell was a cherry demon doing with butterscotch in its generative tract? The eeg should at least be consistent.

The light and the darkness and the bit of red swirled through face and brain, dancing shadow-shapes of zero depth. White and black stretched and strove as though at war and shaped themselves into a silhouette, and the image was of an ebony head with red in the mouth.

"You two-bit, whiteassed, lily-pekkered shit!" the head said.

"Black!" Prior cried. "How good to hear your compliments again! I thought you were dead!"

"I *am* dead, you pale-faced mother-sucker! That whore-demon defucked me, may the Good Lord piss on her."

"The Good Lord didn't get around to it, assuming that He still lives. But if it makes you feel better, I—"

"Shut your farting face, bleachturd! *I'm* dead (that's how I know God *ain't*)—but *you* still got heat in your balls. Get up and fuck that fucker!"

"But the eeg is invulnerable!" Prior bleated.

And woke. The vision of Black was gone, and the eeg was hauling his torso into position for the final ass-sault.

Well, he had Black's posthumous advice, for what it was worth. All he had to do was fuck the fucker (to use the big dead Negro's quaint idiom)—when the eeg had no orifice for the occasion.

Then his mind cleared, helped by a jolt from the demon, and he understood.

The eeg was dragging him arsey-versey past the geyser of ice cream. Prior jerked and twisted and managed to fling one booted foot into that rising column. Instantly his leg was wrenched up, splattering peach ice cream over them both, and he and the demon were hurled sidewise. The eeg's grip was broken, the taffy on Prior's arms cracked with the cold, and he scrambled free again.

He got to his feet and ran. His toes were numb from cold and shock even through the sturdy leather, and his entire leg was coated with peach syrup, but it remained serviceable. He lunged for his pack and pawed through its contents.

The eeg caught up again and resumed hauling, feet-first. It certainly didn't have much imagination. The demon probably had more intellect in its scrotum than in its birdlike skull, at that. But Prior had what he needed: Pipecleaner.

No problem about removing Normal. That member was thoroughly flaccid and half-frozen again under the ice cream. He twisted it off as the demon continued dragging, threw it away and applied the spaghetti-limp substitute, warming it with his two hands. Then he relaxed and concentrated on concupiscence, while his head bumped along the cherry ice. Oubliette, now ... and her sister Tantamount. There was a female who really needed some penile edification, and not in the operating room.

He waited for his opportunity while Pipecleaner swelled into raw macaroni rigidity. Just as the demon got him to the stalagmites, Prior wrenched around, slender phallus erect and eager.

"What do you think of *that*, eggshit?" he demanded.

The eeg's monster penis creaked down like a drawbridge and sniffed. Then the demon began shaking with laughter. Prior's challenging member was no larger in diameter than the slit in the tip of the eeg's phallus.

And as the eeg quaked with its derisive emotion (it probably hadn't had a laugh like that in centuries), Prior took careful aim, braced himself, and thrust. At that slit.

Pipecleaner rammed straight up the giant urethra of the demon.

Prior was fucking the fucker.

The eeg pulled back, amazed; but Prior grabbed handfuls of its disgusting hairy scrotum and hung on. He continued to drive his knitting needle up the cannon-bore.

The eeg tried to scream, but it could only make sounds through its penis, and that was occupied at the moment.

Anyway, it hadn't finished laughing, and it was too stupid to realize that the nature of the joke had changed.

When Prior achieved operative depth he fired off six stitches, knit three and purl three.

Now the eeg's laughter turned to a vast shuddering. Then the massive penis split open, and the rest of the body separated along that same line of cleavage, becoming truly bifurcate. Both halves fell to the floor and dissolved into cherry-wood smoke with a butterscotch mist topping.

Black's final advice had been good. Prior had defeated the last demon in fair genital combat, and now the Spire was his to claim.

Part 4:

Dildo

Chapter 30—Fuck

Tantamount was as lovely as ever. "Why hello, Prior," she exclaimed, as though pleased. "I haven't seen you in months!"

Prior stepped confidently in the door, grasped her by a slender wrist, and drew her into her own living room. There was a considerable bulge at his crotch. "I have what you've always wanted, you charming specialist," he said, patting his too-evident genital region. "I'll give it to you in exchange for my natural penis—dear old faithful 3.97 erect."

She adjusted her hairnet halter with a lift of her classic chin. "But there's nothing I want more than the advancement of science, medicine, and human achievement," she said piously. "Human enlightenment is more important than any other mission. The member you so kindly donated is my essential key to all of these. Once I have collected enough of its unique secretion—"

Prior brought her to the couch and stood her there, his fly seeming ready to burst open. He reached under her skirt to check her posterior equipment. It remained in order: firm, lush buttocks undefended by anything so gross as panties. He sat down and opened his bulging fly at last, revealing the tip of something massive and absolutely rigid.

"Prior, whatever are you—?" she protested.

He ignored this and lifted her onto his lap, so that her skirt spread out and left her cleft open for business at his loin. "Little trick I picked up on the beach, long time ago," he remarked. "Have you any idea how long it's been since I had a real live human-type nubile female woman?"

"Prior, really I don't—" she began. Then the cool, iron-hard horn nudged into her shapely crevice, and there was something about it that silenced her.

"You," he said, "have never been fucked like this, baby."

Her brow wrinkled distastefully. "*Must* you employ such uncouth language? There is appropriate terminology to cover the situation." But she wasn't really upset, for that surprising member of his was caressing her nether regions, promising a fulfillment unlike any she had experienced before, and the contact sent a warm exotic languor radiating out to suffuse her entire body. It was as though she were in love, with him or with his member, and had craved this contact for a thousand years. If deity had a physical manifestation, this was quite possibly it.

"If you have terminology, use it," Prior said harshly. "Tell me what's happening. And no fair peeking!"

She was perplexed. It seemed this was a completely one-sided sexual act from which he received nothing. While she responded to the incredible magic of his member, he was defensive. He had changed, somehow, and not only genitally.

The member moved, sending electrical thrills through her. "Describe it!" he ordered.

She tried. "Your phenomenal penis is stroking my mons pubis," she murmured. "It hardly seems like a prosthetic! Now it is guiding around to my left sulcus labiofemoralis—ooh, that tickles! Don't stop! Now it is crossing my comissura labiorum posterior … sliding along my right labium majus pudenda … my right sulcus nympholabialis … sulcus preputiolabialis … preputum clitordis…"

"You mean it's circling right around your sweating cunt," he said gruffly, "and coming up onto your little man-in-the-boat. Why the hell don't you talk English? So let's just jog your pleasure button a bit, huh?"

She looked at him reproachfully, unable to ascertain the source of his hostility. "Really, those gutter terms—I don't know what they mean." Then the horn got centered and her entire genital region illuminated in response, making her love him anyway. "Massaging my glans clitoridis…"

"Now we'll move on down to pussy headquarters," he said.

The radiating pleasure and promise became almost more than she could bear. She tried once more, desperately, to voice her emotion suitably. "Labium minus pudenda … ostium orethrae … ostium vaginae…" But she was losing her powers of concentration, for that surprising member of his was pushing divinely into her vulva, expanding it, sliding in deeper with an absolutely masculine assurance. An inch, two inches, three, four, five, dilating the entire vaginal tract in a way no woman could ever have experienced before.

"Portio vaginalis cervicis uteri," she breathed, shuddering rapturously. "Ostium uteri…" Then she lost control entirely. "Oh, you're right, Prior. I have never been f— fu— forni—"

"FUCKED!" he said helpfully.

"Fucked like this before," she finished contritely, and quivered all the way into her cavum uteri.

"This," he repeated, "is what you have always desired."

"But science, medicine, human en—" She paused as the pressure of entry abated marginally. "DON'T STOP, Prior!"

"Don't worry, cutie. I won't turn loose your lovely chaste little ass until I've made my deal with you. And to do that, I'll have to infuse some gouts of information, directly into your centers of learning. So hang on—here comes the first!"

The horn wedged so sublimely inside her gouted.

Chapter 31—Spire

I AM THE SPIRE, THE PHALLIC HORN OF PLENTY. FROM ME IS-
SUES THE ETERNAL SPASM OF PROTOPLASM. I WAS CREATED BY THE
ELDEST GOD OF THE GALAXY—KNOWN COLLOQUIALLY BY HIS INITIALS,
EGG—THAT HE MIGHT MORE READILY SATISFY HIS FOURTEEN THOU-
SAND MOST PASSIONATE CONCUBINES AND HIS INNUMERABLE LESS
PASSIONATE HETAERAE AND HIS INCIDENTAL COURTESANS WITHOUT
NEGLECTING HIS LAWFUL WIVES. WITH ME EGG BEGAT ON HIS CHOIC-
EST WIVES ALL THE MORTALS OF THE FIRMAMENT, AND ON HIS CON-
CUBINES HE BEGAT THE DEMONS, AND ON THE REMAINDER HE BEGAT
THE UNCLASSIFIABLES OF EVERY TYPE AND DESCRIPTION. HE EM-
PLOYED A NEW POSITION FOR EACH COPULATION (FOR EGG WAS EVER
ARTISTIC), BEGETTING THE RACES OF MAN BY THE CLOSED, SQUEEZED,
RAISED, PRESSED, HALF-PRESSED, LEANING, ENTWINED, SUSPENDED,
AND WIDE-OPEN POSITIONS; AND THE SPECIES OF ANIMALS BY THE
POSITIONS OF THE MARE, CRAB, COW, DOG, GOAT, DOE, ASS, TIGER,
ELEPHANT, WILD BOAR AND STALLION AND SO ON; AND FOR SPECIAL
OCCASIONS HE EMPLOYED THE POSITIONS OF THE NAIL AND BAMBOO
CLEFT; AND FOR THE RACES AND SPECIES OF DEMONS HE EMPLOYED
ABNORMAL POSITIONS TOO TEDIOUS TO ENUMERATE OR DESCRIBE IN
A SINGLE GOUT. AND WHEN EVERY FEMALE OF THE COSMOS WAS
GRAVID, EGG WAS MINDED TO REST FOR A TIME. BUT IT WAS INCONVE-
NIENT TO TURN ME ON AND OFF OR TO SET ME ASIDE SAFELY, FOR
ANY CREATURE MIGHT TAKE ME AND ABUSE MY POTENCY. SO EGG
CHANGED MY SETTING TO "ENERGY" AND SET ME IN THE CENTER OF
THE ORIGINAL GALAXY, AND WHILE HE SLEPT I SPEWED OUT MORE
ENERGY THAN THE COSMOS HAD YET KNOWN. BUOYED BY MY OUTPUT,
THE EXISTENT SPHERE EXPANDED. WHEN EGG WOKE, THE GALAXY HAD

BECOME A UNIVERSE. AND IT WAS STILL EXPANDING PHENOMENALLY. "THIS IS ON THE VERY VERGE OF GETTING OUT OF HAND!" EGG CRIED, WROTH WITH EXCEEDING WRATH. BUT HE WAS NOT YET INCLINED TO USE ME AGAIN ON HIS MULTIFEROUS FEMALES, SO HE SET ME ON "MAT-TER" WHILE HE CONTEMPLATED THE SITUATION. AND WHILE HE PON-DERED I JETTED FORTH HYDROGEN, THE SIMPLEST ORGANIZED FORM OF MATTER, AND IT FORMED INTO NEBULOUS CLOUDS AND SWIRLS AND SUFFUSED THE UNIVERSE, PROVIDING NOURISHMENT FOR THE DISPLACED STARS AND OBSCURING VASTY TRACTS FROM EGG'S IM-MEDIATE PERCEPTION. AT LAST HE WIPED THE MUCK OF HYDROGEN FROM HIS NOBLE BROW AND DECLARED THAT I WAS TOO MUCH TROUBLE, THOUGH I HAD ONLY DONE MY POTENT DUTY, AND HE SET ME ON "IDLE" AND ABOLISHED ME TO LIMBO AND ASSIGNED FIVE DE-MONIC GUARDS TO PROTECT ME FROM INTRUSION. AND THERE I RE-MAINED A PERIOD, FORGOTTEN. I AM THE SPIRE.

Tantamount blinked prettily and looked at Prior. "Suddenly I know all about the Spire," she said. "But—"

"That was the first gout, delivered as I said straight into your seat of learning. There is more." Prior lifted her off the dribbling member and guided her head down to his crotch.

"Prior, I don't generally make love orally—" she began. But as her mouth opened to speak the words of protest, the tip of his still-won-derfully-solid projection moved in. "This isn't love—it's education," he explained. His hand pressed on the back of her head, forcing it down.

She stiffened as her delicate lips touched the ribbed surface—then sighed around it and took in more. There was something so an-gelically compelling about that contact....

"This is what you have always desired," he repeated firmly.

"Yes!" she exclaimed with her mouth full, and caressed the nox-ious horn lovingly with her tongue. "This is divine. It—it tastes of cherry!"

"All I want," Prior said, "is 3.97. Isn't this a fair exchange?"

She wanted to say YES YES YES, but her rational mind fought down the penis-sponsored urge. "But—" she started.

Then the second gout arrived, and she was far too busy swallow-ing information to talk for a while.

Chapter 32—Eegs

THE FIVE GUARDS WERE GOLEMS, CREATED EXPRESSLY FOR THIS PURPOSE AND ENDOWED WITH FANATIC LOYALTY TO THEIR MISSION. THUS THEY WERE "EXPRESSLY ENDOWED GOLEMS" KNOWN IN THE TRADE AS EEG'S. THE CODE NAME FOR THEIR UNIT WAS "CHERRY TREE," AND THEY ASSUMED THE ASPECT OF COMMENSURATE APPURTE-NANCES. THEY HELD ME IN LIMBO AND DEFENDED MY EXILE FROM ALL INTRUSIONS. PARAGRAPH. (I CAN'T PARAGRAPH IT MYSELF, FOR IT WOULDN'T BE GOUT-SHAPED.) BUT THE EEGS WERE ESSENTIALLY SEXUAL CREATURES AND MY EXILE WAS THEIRS TOO. THEY LONGED FOR THE OLD-FASHIONED INFERNAL ORGIES OR AT LEAST SOME TO-KEN SIN. THREE MALES AND TWO FEMALES—AND WHEN THERE WERE TOO FEW INTRUDERS FOR THEM TO PRACTICE THEIR TALENTS ON, THEY HAD TO INDULGE EACH OTHER. EVERY CENTURY OR SO ONE OF THE FEMALES WOULD CONCEIVE. BUT THE ISSUE, BEING CONTRARY TO THE WORD OF THE ELDEST GOD OF THE GALAXY (NOW ELDEST GOD OF THE UNIVERSE THE GALAXY HAD BECOME, EXALTED BE HIS INACCURATE ACRONYM!), HAD TO BE CONCEALED. THE OFFSPRING COULD NOT BE KILLED, FOR THEY WERE DEMONIC AND IMMORTAL AND NOT SUBJECT TO THE CURSE OF THE CHERRY THAT MADE THEIR ELDERS VULNER-ABLE TO MORTAL EJACULATE. AND SO THESE NEWFOUND DEMONS WERE CAST INTO THE SHAPES OF LIVING CREATURES AND RENDERED IMMOBILE AND PLACED IN SELECTED PARKS AT THE VARIOUS OUTLETS TO THE PASS (FOR SO EGG'S PRIVATE TRAVEL ROUTE WAS TERMED) WHERE THE NATIVES TOOK THEM TO BE STATUES. ONLY WHILE IN THE ACTUAL ACT OF COPULATION WITH LIVING THINGS COULD THESE OUT-CASTS GAIN SOME MEASURE OF THE ANIMATION THEY CRAVED—AND FEW MORTALS CARED TO INDULGE IN COPULATION WITH SUCH STAT-

UES. THE DEMONS THEREFORE BARGAINED FOR SUCH ATTENTIONS BY OFFERING TO ANSWER ANY QUESTION AN OBLIGING MORTAL MIGHT PUT TO THEM. BUT THEY WERE SEVERELY LIMITED IN THE ARTICULATION OF SUCH DISCOURSE. THIS WAS ANOTHER PENALTY FOR BEING THE SPAWN OF ADULTEROUS EEGS. ONLY BY THE INFUSION OF LEGITIMATE PROTOPLASM COULD THEY BE RENDERED FULLY ANIMATE THEMSELVES. I AM THE SPIRE.

The horn withdrew from Tantamount's mouth, and red fluid drooled from between her sparkling white teeth. "Suddenly I know all about certain statues," she said, licking the overflow from her red lips. "Those horrible statues behind my sister's clinic. But—"

"That was the second gout," Prior explained. "There is more." He guided her into a prone position on the couch, and lifted her skirt out of the way so that her full, resilient buttocks showed in all their clean white splendor. He brought a little more of the member into view. It was still as hard as horn, and though narrow at the tip its girth increased toward the base. Its aperture was not a slit but a round hole, surprisingly large for a penis.

"That phallus does not have the most esthetic configuration," she said, glancing over her shoulder at it. "But every time it touches me I palpitate, and when it ejaculates I have visions and I feel so good..."

"This is what you have always desired," he said once more.

"But my life work—"

He positioned himself and hauled up her generous posterior so that her smooth, perfectly molded cleft showed taut. He spread the silky flesh of her labia, nudging in the horn.

"Yes, yes!" she breathed breathlessly.

"Let's do this right," he said as he inched the horn in. "This is the position of the Cow, according to the ancient erotic texts of India. Let's say I'm the bull, and this is the bullhorn. So moo, cow, moo!"

The caress of that horny member unnerved her with its incipient thrills, but she still had female human pride. "Prior, this is ridiculous! Why must you spoil—"

He began to withdraw, and the promise abated.

"Moo! Moo!" she cried, alarmed.

The retreat ceased, but the advance did not resume. "But I'm not sure I want to fuck a cow at the moment. It's too bovine, know what I mean? Let's make it the position of the Dog. How about it? Would you make a good female dog?"

"This is disgusting! Absolutely animalistic! I won't—"

He recommended the strategic withdrawal.

"I'm a bitch! I'm a bitch!" she screamed.

"Funny. You don't *sound* like a bitch.

"Arf! Wuf! Ho-o-owl!"

She was getting the message.

"But maybe the ass is better," he said thoughtfully. "A nice, bray-ing, donkey-type ass."

She was silent. The horn hesitated inside her, then began to retr—

"I'm a piece of ass!" she cried.

"But I feel more like a wild boar, so—"

"I'm a pig! Oink, oink!"

"Then again, maybe an elephant—"

"Anything you want! Please, Prior—"

"Why," he said curiously, "you sound almost as if you want some-thing...."

"Enter and ejaculate! Don't torture me!"

He cupped one hand behind an ear. "I'm not certain I compre-hend the terminology."

"Complete the fornication!"

"Eh?"

"Fuck me! FUCK ME!"

"Oh, all right, if you feel that way." He eased the horn on in to jog the eager cervix. "Here comes the third gout, elephant ass bitch!"

And the third gout came, driving out the remnants of the first gout as new grease from the greasegun drives out old.

Chapter 33—Eggs

AFTER SEVERAL THOUSAND MILLENNIA THE CHERRY TREE EEG DEMONS (SEE GOUT NO. 2 FOR RATIONALE OF NOMENCLATURE) REALIZED THAT I COULD BE EMPLOYED FOR THEIR PURPOSE, FOR I COULD PRODUCE THE MORTAL PROTOPLASM THEY DESIRED AND I HAD NOT ACTUALLY BEEN TURNED OFF. AND SO THEY FORNICATED WITH ME UPON OCCASION—TWO OR THREE TIMES PER CENTURY—AND FROM EACH SUCH UNION A LIVING EEGLET WAS CONCEIVED AND BIRTHED AS AN EGG. THESE EGGS WERE STORED AT THE BORDERS OF LIMBO AND FORGOTTEN. BUT THE STRAIN OF SUCH POTENCY ON THE DEMONIC SYSTEMS WAS SUCH THAT THEIR GENITAL SECRETIONS WERE ADVERSELY AFFECTED. THUS THE CHERRY DEMONS DEVELOPED BUTTERSCOTCH-FLAVORED EJACULATE, MUCH TO THEIR CHAGRIN. PARAGRAPH. EVENTUALLY A CACHE OF THESE EEG EGGS WAS DISCOVERED BY A SPACEFARING MORTAL, WHO ASCERTAINED THEIR SINGULAR NATURE AND WHOLESALED THEM ON THE BLACK MARKET. SOON INFANT EEGS WERE SCATTERED ALL OVER THE UNIVERSE, FOR REMOVAL FROM LIMBO AND CONTACT WITH MORTAL FLESH STIMULATED THEIR HATCHING AND GROWTH. NATURALLY THEY PROCEEDED TO WREAK SUCH MISCHIEF AS THEY MIGHT. THIS WAS ENTIRELY AGAINST DEMONIC PRINCIPLE, FOR IT SIGNALED THE END OF THE PROPER SEPARATION OF MAGIC AND SCIENCE. BUT THE SMUGGLING CONTINUED. I AM THE SPIRE.

"And now I know about eeg eggs," Tantamount said. "This is astonishing."

"It's all leading up to the deal we are about to make," Prior said confidently. "I have what you've always wanted."

"Yes," she said, starting to turn over.

"Not so fast, bitch ass!" He caught inside her thigh, squeezing the fine firm flesh between thumb and fingers until she winced. Then he stroked his hand between her lush buttocks, bearing down on her rectum. "Now for this next number—"

"Prior," she protested, squirming. "What—"

"Now is the month of Maying," he sang, stroking her flinching sphincter again. "When merry lads are playing, fa-la-la-la-la—"

Tantamount tried to straighten out, but he hooked his other arm around her voluptuous hips and held her there, rear pointed up. He scooped a little clear grease from her vagina where it overflowed and rubbed it generously over her anus. "Each with his bonnie lass," he sang, thumbing some of the lubricant into the target hole. "A-dancing on her ass, fa-la-la-la—"

"Surely you don't intend to practice anal intercourse?" she asked, shocked.

"This isn't practice, innocent baby. I'm thoroughly experienced, thanks to the tour you started me on."

"But I never indulge in perversive exploits! It isn't—"

"You don't consider it perversive to hack off a man's living, fucking penis and crucify it in a laboratory?"

"So that's why you're so angry! Prior, how can you bear such a grudge for such a little—"

"It may be little, but it's *mine*. 3.97 erect. I want it back."

"But I need it for the advancement of—"

She silenced as the great horn centered on her attractively puckered rectum and nosed determinedly within. The breadth of it distended her sphincter and the hollow tip of it probed far into her virgin bowel, a hypodermic ready to inject. "Who would have suspected it would feel so good!" she murmured wantonly.

"This horn always feels divine,"' he said. He hesitated again. "Next time you feel like stealing a man's—"

"Never again!" she cried.

"Cross your heart?"

"Cross my fucking heart!"

He nodded, satisfied. The fourth gout flooded her colon.

Chapter 34—Mountain

NOW IT CAME TO PASS THAT EGG LEARNED OF THE EEG EGGS (IT SEEMS ONE WAS INADVERTENTLY POACHED FOR HIS BREAKFAST) AND REALIZED THAT NOT ONLY WAS SOMETHING AMISS, HIS ACRONYM HAD BEEN PROFANED. SO HE BANISHED ME TO AN UNINHABITED WORLD, AND MY GUARDIANS WITH ME, AND DECREED THAT HENCEFORTH I SHOULD SPOUT ONLY LUDICROUS SUBSTANCE. ABOUT THAT TIME ONE OF THE BACKWARD PLANETS HAD INVENTED ICE CREAM (A NOXIOUS CONFECTION OF ANIMAL MAMMARY MILK AND VEGETABLE SUGAR, DEVIOUSLY FLAVORED AND CHILLED TO SEMI-SOLIDITY), SO HE STARTED ME OFF WITH THAT, MY PENALTY FOR MILLENNIA OF LOYAL SERVICE. NATURALLY I PRODUCED ONLY THE FINEST GRADE OF EVERY FLAVOR AND TYPE—BUT THERE WAS NO ONE PRESENT TO CONSUME IT. GRADUALLY A MOUNTAIN OF IT FORMED ABOVE ME, YET I COULD NOT DESIST WITHOUT A SPECIFIC DIRECTIVE, AND THE DEMONS WERE NO LONGER EMPOWERED FOR THAT. ONLY WHEN SOME INTREPID MORTAL CONQUERED THE GUARDIAN EEGS (BY REAMING THEIR DEMON ASSES) AND PROVIDED A NEW DIRECTIVE COULD I MODIFY MY OUTPUT. FINALLY SUCH A MAN CAME. I AM THE SPIRE. FUCK YOU, SISTER—YOU'RE MY MILLIONTH-GENERATION DESCENDANT.

"Prior!" she exclaimed. "You conquered the Spire. The phallic horn of plenty!"

"It is," he murmured, "up your ass."

"Help! I've been stuffed with ice cream!"

He withdrew the tip of the Spire and watched the yellowish substance ooze out of her flaccid rectum. "Not exactly. I switched formulae each time. Standard-potency human ejaculate for the first gout that will make you a mother in just about nine months—"

"No!" she cried, appalled. "I took Precautions!"

"So did some of those wives and concubines. But the Spire has never had a failure. It is, you might say, the irresistible force."

She turned over now, stricken. "Gravid! And I'm not even married!"

"The second gout was cherry ice cream, of course," he continued imperturbably. "Petroleum jelly for the third—"

"WHAT?!"

"Well, I know we'd be needing some lubricant for the fourth, so—"

Tantamount squirted from his grasp, assisted in the maneuver by the leaking lubricant, and stood on the floor quivering beautifully with fury. "Of all the—you, you—you MAN, you!"

"But for the fourth gout I have stuffed you with what you have always most desired. That's why it felt so good."

"But all I have ever desired is science, medicine, and—" she began plaintively.

"Precisely. And how do you propose to achieve all this?"

"I was setting up my laboratory to perform an exhaustive analysis of your penile smegma, to ascertain—"

Prior removed the Spire from his crotch where it had been fastened to his attachment-base, and set it upright in the center of the room. It was about a foot long, horn-shaped, with a gentle column of steam rising from its narrow aperture. "All you needed," he said gravely, "was enough of that unique smegma to spread out for your multiple tests. And 3.97 can't have been producing much, because naturally it doesn't like being isolated in the lab, fuckless. So you haven't gotten far, have you, saving mankind from a fate worse than abstinence?"

Her full breasts shook. "But in time—"

"You don't need time. You need smegma. Well, you have it now."

"I—?"

"Shit a little, Emdee. Find out what I put in there, that last gout."

Dazed, she squatted and strained. Her bottom extruded a waxy ribbon of substance. She caught some of it on her finger, brought it to her face, frowned and touched her tongue to it. "Smegma! You mean—?"

"Cheese, sister, cheese. My very own formula, proof against all venereal disease except amputation. All yours now."

"Smegma!" she exclaimed, brightening visibly. "How wonderful! There must be half a pound of it in me. I must conserve it all!" And she began straining in earnest.

Prior smiled indulgently. "Don't bother. I am giving you the Spire, set to that formula. It will produce as much as you need—maybe even more than enough." He twiddled with the great horn, and it began spouting more of the waxy stuff. The first sustained gout hit the ceiling and splashed down all over the living room, and more followed in a steady stream. It was a yellow fountain.

"Oh!" Tantamount exclaimed, running over and trying to catch it all in her hands. She was like a child in a candy store. "It's raining smegma! Oh joy!"

"Courtesy of Egg's cosmic dildo, the source of all potency." Prior sighed with satisfaction. "Now I'm going over to your lab and I'm taking back my penis—3.97 erect. It's a fair bargain. Have fun." He waved as he left.

She had already forgotten him. She was in smegma heaven. The stuff was pouring on her head, and she was smearing it over her exquisite body as though it were soap, transfixed by delight. "All I can ever use!" she cried. "I'll eat it, drink it, sleep in it—"

It took Prior about half an hour to get his precious penis disconnected from the lab setup and reconnected to his socket, but finally it stood proud and not too tall at his loin. Now it was just over four inches, because the socket added to its length, but he remained well satisfied. A long (or more correctly, short) lost friend had been recovered, and they were going to have a fucking good time together.

Of course he would keep the alternate members too, since variety was the spice of sex. And he would have to drop in on Oubliette to obtain a special fitting, so that he could handle the little errand he owed Black. A certain bunch of fat crooked policemen were going to get screwed—simultaneously. Compliments of a late noble man.

As he left the house he saw yellowish material pouring thickly out the window. It was excess smegma overflowing the confines of Tantamount's living room.

Prior chuckled. No one but he could turn off the Spire or change its setting, and he intended to lose himself. So unless the Eldest God of the Galaxy became aware of the situation and interceded, Tantamount would have more than enough.

In fact, this was the beginning of the formation of Mt. Smegma.

Author's Note

Every book has its story, and this one more so than most. First a bit of history.

Back in 1969 I was constantly looking for markets, as like most writers I had more of a problem getting material published than I did writing it. Other speculative genre writers tried erotica, and I had word that a particular editor at ESSEX HOUSE was doing some really fantastic stuff. So I queried, and received several books as samples. I read them, and they were indeed fantastic erotica. By that I mean they were in the erotic genre, with plenty of hot sex, but also in the fantasy or science fiction genre—the sort of thing you didn't see in standard genre print, which was traditionally notable in its paucity of romance and complete absence of sex. Yes, I could do this sort of writing.

So I started writing *3.97 Erect*, the title referring to the length of the protagonist's diminutive erect penis. It moved well, as I had him encounter a succubus at the beach and discover with her the remarkable anti-venereal-disease property of his smegma. Then he ran afoul of Tantamount Emdee, the luscious idealistic unscrupulous lady doctor and researcher, and lost his marvelous little member.

About that time I lost my prospective market. The innovative editor had been abruptly fired and the fantastic line shut down. My promise had been amputated in much the manner of Prior's penis. So I left the novel and went on to more conventional genre writing. But it bugged me, and a year later I returned to finish it, on general principles.

It was a challenge, for I had run out of my initial idea. What could I write that was as fantastic as what I had written? I checked my file of unused ideas, and found one that hadn't fit anywhere. It wasn't erotic, but perhaps it could be adapted. Thus came to be Mount Icecream, with its motley cast of characters—how did you like that black and white horse sleigh haul down the slope?—and from that derived the profane conclusion of the novel as I labored to work out the explanation for that mountain. I was concerned that readers would fathom the completely different elements of the story, but I never had a comment or complaint. Perhaps, as with sausages, it is best that a writer's sources of story not be inspected too closely.

So the novel was done—without a market. It was no good for the traditional porno publishers because of its fantastic element, and the way it violated their taboos, such as referring directly to venereal disease, feces, and the fact that a man *can't* just service women in rapid order without limitation. At one point a traditional publisher, BANTAM BOOKS, considered it; their editor said that it received several rather sweaty readings there, but they concluded that they didn't want to get this solidly into the erotic genre. Another editor was interested, but then found a better job at another publisher that didn't do erotica, where he worked with a new writer named Dean Koontz. So my loss was Dean's gain, and he went on to better things. So the novel languished, a victim of its nature and sheer chance.

Until more than fifteen years later when Charles Platt saw it listed in my bibliography and asked to see it. He liked it, and set up his own publisher to publish it, BLACK SHEEP PRESS. He wasn't satisfied with the title, and after some dialog came up with *Pornucopia*, which seemed ideal. But he couldn't get a printer to print it; even those who claimed to have no taboos suddenly balked when they saw the manuscript. Unable to publish it, BLACK SHEEP went out of business. But he did find another prospective publisher, Phil Gurlik, who set up TAFFORD starting with this novel, and which subsequently did several others of mine. So that worked out well enough in the end.

TAFFORD's *Pornucopia* sold slowly but well; it had legs, in the industry parlance. Actually it was what was between the legs that counted. It ran through three printings despite being restricted to readers age 21 or over. I am privately pleased that over the years I have received no complaints about its content, either that it failed to deliver what it promised, or that some child got hold of it and freaked out. (Well, I did have a teen girl correspondent who somehow sneaked a peek. "Oh my lost innocence!" she lamented.) So our restraints on sales seem to have been effective. I really don't want to alienate my readers, but neither do I want to be limited to "safe" material.

Then TAFFORD shut down, and we sought an online publisher. We found one, ELECTRIC BOOKWORM—that went out of business before getting the novel online. Back to square one. Meanwhile the novel had become rare, while demand continued, so that at one point it was pirated, and at another readers were being soaked $150 or more per copy. Such a price for such a dirty book! I wanted to stop this, because I don't like having my dedicated readers ripped off by scalpers.

Thus we came again to a new person, Daniel Reitz, who had to start his own publisher in order to do it (established publishers quickly turn conservative) and MUNDANIA PRESS came to be. That accounts for the present edition, which I went over and edited slightly for punctuation, mainly the elimination of surplus exclamation points, and I added chapter titles. We promise not to rip off readers with ludicrous prices, and we lowered the age limit a bit, as readers seem to be getting more mature earlier and societal restraints have been loosening. So now anyone age 18 or over can get it. But it remains a dirty book; there has never been any misrepresentation on that score. Do not send a gift-wrapped copy to your maiden aunt or parish priest.

If this works out, I'll write a sequel, *The Magic Fart*, that picks up where *Pornucopia* leaves off and takes Prior Gross to new and gloriously offensive erotic and scatologic depths. I have had a few more wild notions, and will see now they work out. There's bound to be a stench.

And no, I really doubt that Hollywood is likely to make a movie of either novel.

About the Author

Piers Anthony is one of the world's most prolific and popular authors. His fantasy Xanth novels have been read and loved by millions of readers around the world, and have been on the *New York Times* Best Seller list many times. Although Piers is mostly known for fantasy and science fiction, he has written several novels in other genres as well, including historical fiction, martial arts, and horror. Piers lives with his lovely wife in a secluded woods hidden deep in Central Florida.

Do you want to learn more about Piers Anthony?

Piers Anthony's official website is HI PIERS at **www.hipiers.com**, where he publishes his bi-monthly online newsletter. HI PIERS also has a section reviewing many of the online publishers and self-publishing companies for your reference if you are looking for a non-traditional solution to publish your book.

Piers Anthony's largest fan-based website is The Compleat Piers Anthony at **www.piers-anthony.com**. The Compleat Piers Anthony contains extensive information about all the books and stories that Piers has written, as well as up-to-date information about forthcoming books.

Mundania Press LLC

www . mundania . com
books @ mundania . com

THE CHROMAGIC SERIES

1,000 years ago Earth colonized the planet Charm. But the population of Charm is now far removed from their ancient ancestors. Technology has been lost over the years but the people have something better—Magic!

Charm is a world covered by volcanoes, each erupting a different color of magic. Everything within a particular Chroma becomes that color. Plants, animals, insects, and even humans all become one color and can perform that color of magic. Traveling is dangerous because a person leaving their native Chroma home can no longer perform their color magic.

In **KEY TO HAVOC**, Havoc is a barbarian living in a non-Chroma village, where no one has magic. As a boy, he rescued a dragon that rewarded him with special magic; to sense pending danger. His gift becomes more valuable than he can imagine as he is suddenly drafted and forced to become the new king of the planet. He must perform his duties or be executed for treason. To make matters worse, the assassin who killed the former king is now after Havoc!

> Hardcover—0-9723670-7-1
> Trade Paperback—0-9723670-6-3
> eBook—1-59426-000-1

In **KEY TO CHROMA**, With the help of the God-like Glamors, Havoc and his companions must set off in search of seven mysterious ikons to attempt to learn the secret of the Changelings ... a secret that could answer all of Havoc's questions, or lead him to his doom.

> Hardcover—0-9723670-7-1
> Trade Paperback—0-9723670-6-3
> eBook—1-59426-000-1

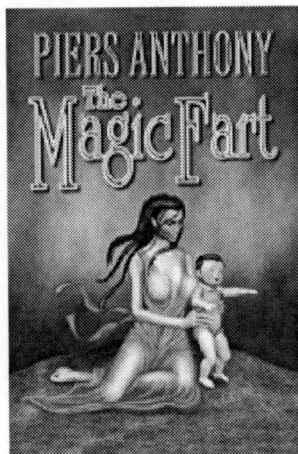

Printed in the United States
119364LV00011B/152/A